'Time means nothing when you are eternal. Everything that happens at the same time. All possibilities exist.'

KARMA THE ASSASSIN

BOOK ONE

D1737339

COLLECTOR'S EDITION

Karma the assassin, honoured be thy name

'Do you remember a moment in your life when you were complete – like in the afterglow of the best sex of your life, but better?

You know the one, when your bodies talk, you touch, smell, taste, dive into the wetness, with your full breath, with no limits.

The ecstasy of completely dissolving once, twice, again; the sounds, animal, raw, hungry. Wanting to melt skin, entwine, get closer than a heartbeat, consume, disappear, fuck.

The afterglow of the best sex of your life - that feeling of deep peace, knowing your place, love, kindness – that state is how we lived and felt every day of our lives.

Men led with heart. Women led with power.

We were what you call promiscuous.

All was right with the world.'

Letters

Table of Contents

Chapter 1 The way we were

Rania

The temple stood on a hill overlooking the valley of the gods. Our river flowed lazy, never really contained by its banks, reflecting the sun's rays at sunset; bursting with abundance.

Our orchard sprawled on the slope behind the temple. A winding path led through the layered terraces into the valley, each terrace useful – herbs on this one, our food on this one, rituals performed during solstice on this one.

The air, perfumed year round by some flower or other in bloom, healed the sick that travelled from far and wide to be seen and blessed by my hands. I could sense them coming; weary, hopeful, or with the intention to die in peace.

We prepared for them; rooms with fresh linen, fruit from our trees, water from our fountain. I would walk down to the herb garden and touch and smell a few stems, making sure I carried their trace on me before meeting my patient. Watched my daughter, Leena, do the same.

The diagnostic method was passed on from healer to apprentice since the foundation of the temple, three centuries ago.

'The beings that come to us, Leena,' I say as we pick the freshest stems to prepare a herbal concoction for the fertility rituals, 'are not at ease with themselves and their environment. They have lost their balance and no longer live in harmony. Your foremost task is to give them a space of non-judgement and acceptance.'

'I understand, Rania.'

'First, observe,' I continue. 'The clothes they wear; the expression on their face; the way their body sits, or slouches, or lies in bed. The colouring on their face and hands. Are there any dark circles? Veins? Are their eyes clear or obscured by pain?' I pause. 'Look at me.'

Leena stands, taking me in. Her lanky frame moves slightly. She connects to her core and opens up space and silence for the two of us, using her entire body.

'Tell me what you see and how.'

She answers in statements, not questioning her knowing. 'You have your menses; it's your third day. You did not sleep well last night. Are you troubled by dreams?'

'Correct.'

'What did you dream of Rania?'

'It's too soon to tell, my dear. Your seeing is very good. Would you like to take on our patients by yourself today?'

'Oh yes!'

'Can I come with you?' one of our charges, Sonia, six years old, had been sitting behind a rosemary bush, listening in on us. The bush covered her completely, only her head was visible behind it as she stood on tiptoe. Her whole face beamed with excitement.

'Sonia, who are you hiding from?' I ask.

'Aanaka doesn't let me play with her. Can I come with Leena to see the patients?'

Aanaka the foundling.

'Only if you don't interrupt her work.'

'Can I tell them my stories?'

'Happy stories, yes?' I pierce her eyes with mine, willing her to obey.

She mumbles, 'Yes, Rania.' Takes Leena's hand.

They walk off into the back of the temple, where our guests rest in rooms of healing. I turn away to watch the valley. It spreads out as far as the eye can see. Villages are perched on the banks of the river, framed by fields of wheat and barley. Cows, sheep, and horses move slowly on pastures separated by nutmeg trees. The forests begin to my left. Far to my right mountains stand guard at the entrance to the desert.

I trust Leena to know how to treat our patients; how to unwind the tightness in their muscles, let them be. Allow them to show her where the imbalance is, how it started, what is its purpose. She is thirteen now. Old enough to take on more responsibility.

Sometimes our patients thank us and leave ready to face life again. Other times they die, smiling. Wondering when they'll be reborn.

A healer's craft begins at birth and is honed by years of training. Leena's gift shines so brightly, even the birds sense it. They come to her with their broken beaks or claws, trusting her to make them well.

It was one of the birds who told us about the soldiers.

But wait, not yet. Let's not remember that yet.

I want to show you what the world was like when we were whole. Before men started learning about power.

Thirteen priestesses at the temple. Six charges in our care.

We called each other sisters but our ties ran deeper than blood, connecting us through an understanding of existence, an agreement on our purpose, and unconditional love.

From tribes scattered across Gaia, we gathered together to serve Her; weaving a rich tapestry of worship, each thread our own essence entwined; ever expanding.

Our eldest, Marwa, leathery face ageless, symbols of power tattooed across her forehead and cheeks, sent her spirit out into the world searching for new apprentices every year. Her body slept while on this journey and it was my task to care for it until her return.

Marwa came to me in a dream, many years ago, when I was finishing my training at the Springs of She. Grey hair tied back in a bun, short in stature, wiry, crone's laughter in her eyes. Dressed in a black woollen skirt embroidered with roses, once bright, now faded with age and wash. She wouldn't let Mina, our keeper of coin, buy her a new one. 'I gained the knowledge of existence while making this skirt,' she said. 'I don't need a new one.'

Her blouse gathered at the neck, green thread tracing motifs of delicate spring leaves in cross stitching across the front, back, and sleeves. A grey woollen shawl covered her shoulders. Beads of jade and amethyst, bone and wood clinked as she danced on fields of grain.

She saw the past, present, and future at once - everything you could be in all the choices you make.

I am certain she could have commanded me to come and be a priestess at this temple. It would have been an honour to accept. Instead, she teased and cajoled and took me to the deepest forests of the North where we ran wild every night, as soon as I fell asleep.

During the last night of my initiation, she brought me here. We stood just outside the entrance doors basking in warmth and love. I saw women and girls playing under light streaming from the sun in golden rays. Suddenly, the ground started shaking, splintered apart, and swallowed the temple whole. I was left alone, looking into the abyss. Calling out names I did not remember when I awoke.

I had forgotten about that dream.

It reminded me that nothing lasts forever again last night.

I stood on the brink of the same abyss.

The darkness called out my name and -

I followed, gladly.

Mina

I stand by Bianca watching the girls play. We laugh as Sia jumps out from behind a rosebush and stops Aanaka in her tracks, pulling at her braid. Baby Ruth, arms out, is chasing Deena who is pretending to run to keep with the little one's pace, catching her just as she's about to fall. They giggle and squeal and cartwheel flowing from one game to the next.

'I sent out a messenger with a note to the cloth seller this morning.' I say to Bianca who is distracted by the noise and looks like she wants to join them.

'Ah yes? When is he coming?' She asks.

'First thing tomorrow. I need your help to decide what fabric to buy and how much of it we need.'

'That's easy. Sia will need something sturdy, linen, very thick. Aanaka really brought her out of her shell hasn't she?' She asks.

'Yes, she has. I'm glad she's not spending all her days in the library any longer.'

'It's not good for her to study so much without having some time to run about. All that mathematics. I'm surprised her head doesn't hurt.'

'Ha. She's using it, you know.' I say defensively.

'Really?'

'Yes. Those two have solemnly promised to build a shed.'

'When was that?'

'Last year. I'm still waiting for the drawings.'

'How will they build us a shed if Aanaka is down in the villages all the time, helping them with their houses?'

'It takes time, I suppose.'

'Well, no matter. Linen for them both.'

'Linen. One bolt should cover it. Deena?'

'Sweet Deena. She's following me around everywhere these days! I have to make sure she's not peeking when I'm entertaining men.'

'When are you going to start teaching her?'

'In a few years.' She pauses, thinking. 'You know, she has a skill at peace keeping. Can we get someone to teach her diplomacy and rhetoric?'

'Yes. I'll arrange for it. What dress does she need?'

'Silk. She loves silk.'

'One bolt of silk.' I make a note of it on a piece of parchment. 'She can choose it. Now, Leena.'

'Leena, so gifted, isn't she?'

'Bianca, I have a lot to do. Can we just decide on the wares really quickly?'

In a soothing tone, Bianca replies. 'All right. Don't get into a state. Leena needs something with pockets, wool. Oh and also silk, for her initiation ceremony.'

'They will both have to agree on the same bolt. Should be fun to witness.' I say. 'Now Sonia.'

Bianca giggles. 'Have you heard her latest story? The one about a cloud that fell in love with the sun and melted to let it shine through. Oh, don't roll your eyes! My favourite is – listen. She told me in confidence; had me promise not to tell the others.' She touches Mina on the forearm. 'One of a boy who loved a girl and made her a garland of flowers - her favourite, daffodils - because he wanted her to smile.

She hadn't smiled in a long time because she missed her mother, who disappeared one day. Strange story. Why would her mother just disappear?'

'Her stories are more than what they seem, you know. Even Marwa agrees.'

'I suppose. Marwa does know a lot. Although she won't let you get her out of that old skirt.'

'Who knows, maybe she'll teach one of them about that skirt someday. Now Ruth.'

'Aw. Baby Ruth. I love her. She's so precious!'

'Bianca, please.'

'If you ask me, she can have any dress she wants. Her favourite colour is green.'

'It looks like important decisions will have to be made tomorrow. I can't wait to see how they all cooperate. Now, I'm off to the granary to check on supplies for the festivities. Thank you. Will you be there for the merriment?'

'I wouldn't miss it for the world.'

Diana

I have a bad feeling about this. It's a tightening in my stomach that no amount of food or water can pacify. It started a few months ago, with one of the girls, Sonia.

Sonia likes to keep Leena company as she goes about tending to the herb garden or feeding a stray fox. Leena has infinite patience for her stories.

One day I caught Leena asking Sonia to tell her the story of the sparrow. She was holding one gently, stroking its beak. She wanted to know why it broke its wing. Sonia was silent for a moment.

'It broke its wing to show you how you die.' She said.

'Oh I wouldn't die from a broken arm. Rania would heal me, silly. No one dies from a broken arm.'

At that moment, Aanaka's laughter pierced the air as she ran up the hill arms out, flailing, being chased by Sia.

'I found you, I found you!' She shouted. 'You have to stop.'

They both disappeared into the temple. We heard a crash and an immediate hush.

Then Mina, sighing:

'Oh Aanaka, it's the third vase this week. If you don't like them just say so and we'll put them somewhere else. You don't have to destroy all of them.'

'I'm so very sorry, I didn't mean to,' explained Aanaka, breathless. 'Sia was chasing me and I had to hide and I wanted to get to the corner and hide behind it but then I couldn't stop in time and then it just crashed into me, this vase.'

'The vase crashed into you.'

'Yes. It was very painful. See? It even scratched my elbow.'

'All right, go ask Leena to take a look at your elbow. This needs to be cleaned before dinner, understood?'

'Yes. Ow, my poor elbow.'

Aanaka walked over to Leena and Sonia, holding her elbow, dragging her leg behind for added effect. Sia giggled.

'You made Mina very angry I think. I hope she lets you have a new dress for the ceremony.'

It made me laugh. The girls always made me laugh. But my laughter was poisoned by a bitterness that I never felt before. I felt pain and I could not explain it away. Rania had no explanation for it. But she took my worry seriously and asked Marwa to take me on a vision journey.

Marwa laid me in a circle of stones on one of the terraces. On top of one of the stones, engraved with ancient symbols, she laid a fire and kept it burning for three days.

When I finally opened my eyes she said. 'Child. Whatever you saw is yours to know, not yours to share.'

'But Marwa, I must warn them.'

'No.' She answers sharply. 'Keep silent.'

'Marwa. We must prepare. We must ask for help.'

'Child. You cannot prevent the inevitable. If you warn them, you will poison them with the same fear you feel. Stay with your fear. It is yours.' She looks me in the eye. 'Your fear is yours.'

With that, she left me alone. I spent days in communion with the goddess, hoping for guidance. None came.

My sisters. There is nothing similar to our way of life in your world. But I know your cells remember other lifetimes where you too were a priestess, serving the Goddess.

Our temple was a place of learning, healing, and celebration. Foreigners journeyed to ask for blessings; kings journeyed asking for divination; women journeyed asking for children; men journeyed asking for love.

My sisters. Offerings from devotees and apprentices' families accumulated in our coffers and we were able to send caravans to the east and to the west, to the north and to the south, exchanging goods and knowledge with other temples. We travelled and learned new languages and the new ways of the world.

My sisters. I loved them like you love your children and your soulmates. I knew them and they knew me. The knowing that comes with intuition and years of living side by side and of bonds of love that went from one to another to another in an interwoven web of kindness and strength and acceptance. Like my heart that gave me life, they gave me a home and a place and a purpose.

Together, we were complete.

'The yearning for wholeness is the guiding light that will bring you home.'

Letters

Daniel

Sonia is skipping beside Leena, following her into the living quarters. She is faster than her but doesn't know where to go so she stops, comes back and falls in line with Leena's pace.

'Leena, what do you have to do after you observe the patient?' She asks.

'Come close to them.' She answers.

'And then?'

'Observe how they change.'

'And then?'

'Ask them questions.'

'What questions?'

'Ask where it hurts.'

'And then?'

Leena gets a bit impatient:

'And then listen, and then examine, and then give them medicine to sleep and then tickle them.'

Sonia stops, surprised.

'What? How?'

'Like this.'

Tinkling laughter echoing off temple walls as Leena chases Sonia whose giggles are like bubbles bursting. They stop before a wooden door with a bronze carved handle.

'Shh. Are you ready to help me with the first patient?'

'Yes.'

She opens the door slowly. It creaks a bit. There's an old man lying in bed, facing the wall. He turns to look at the girls. Sonia hides behind Leena, peeking.

'Good morning, Daniel.'

'Good morning. Rania's not here, eh? I must be almost ready to go home. My wife misses me too much, she comes to me in dreams now. And who's this?' He asks, sitting up.

'I'm Sonia.' She says shyly.

'Hello Sonia. Are you a healer too?'

'No, I am curious.'

'Well, not much mystery here, I am simply old.'

'You're like a leaf.'

'Like a leaf, eh?'

'Yes. Leena, can I tell a story?'

'Go on.'

Daniel breaks into a broad smile. 'A storyteller, are you? How wonderful! Please, tell me a story.'

Sonia begins shyly. 'Well there once was a leaf, you know. It was not a very big leaf, nor a small one. It budded in spring on one of the branches of a willow growing by the river. It opened, and stretched, and changed colours, and was very happy with the sun playing. The sun made it very warm and transparent, and when the wind came it danced together with the other leaves. For many days it played and danced and sang in the sun and was washed by the rain.' Stopping, she looks up at Daniel, changing her tone. 'Then the wind became colder and colder, and the sun did not stay in the sky as long as before, and it changed colours again. It became more difficult to dance because it was not as strong. And one day the wind blew a little harder and it broke free from its branch singing so happily – it was such a new sensation! It fell into the water and the river took it to a bank to sleep with the other leaves. And a new leaf will be born in its spot next spring.' Hands fall to her sides, she goes quiet.

The old man looks at her while Leena pours water into a clay cup and lets three drops fall from a vial on the table. Finally, he says.

'I did enjoy dancing very much, Sonia.' He sighs, taking the cup from Leena's hands. Drinks it fully and hands it back to her. 'Maybe it is time for me to go to sleep. What a good storyteller you are!'

'I like stories.'

Leena says quietly. 'Rest, Daniel, I'll see you in the evening. Come, Sonia.'

They leave, closing the door softly behind them.

'Oh how my wife will miss me.' Whispers Daniel to himself.

'Listen, carefully, to what people say. Feel what they don't say.'

Letters

Chapter 2 The new men

Titus

'I won't do it! I won't go on an expedition with that pompous ass.'

'I'm afraid you have no choice, Titus.'

The senator, sprawled on a settee on the veranda overlooking the city, watched his son pacing before him, agitated and irritated. He stopped, looking at his father's proud face. It was lined with wrinkles, bitter at the corners of his mouth, heavy with excess wine and food. The whites of his eyes yellow, tinged with liver trouble; grey hair impeccably combed and oiled. It was late spring, the light silk tunic barely covered his body. His skin was loose and moved unpleasantly on his neck, arms, and chest as he picked grapes from a bunch and dropped them into his mouth one by one.

I never want to get old, thought Titus with a shudder. It's disgusting.

'Tell me again why I should go.' He says out loud.

'Shoo! Get away from here. Leave the wine and go; go!' The senator gestures with both arms at a slave boy. The boy runs away as fast as his legs will carry him. 'Don't let me see you again until I call you' he shouts after him. He turns back to face the young man. 'Titus, my son, why must you try my patience so? The more times I repeat the plan, the greater the danger that we'll be overheard and it will come to nothing.'

'Humor me one last time. If I have to go to the gods know where with that blithering idiot, at least give me one good reason.' He insists.

'Family. There is no greater reason than that. Your sister married well, granting us more influence in the senate. Now it's your turn to contribute. Unite your men with Regulus, be under his command and secure land and possessions for us. Show the king you can be trusted to bring new territory to Rome and glory to the empire, and he will shower you with honours. He might even make you a general in his army.'

'Be under Regulus' command? Are you mad? I'd rather be dead.' He says angrily.

'Titus, listen to me. You will both be far away from home. You will face untold dangers from the savages.' He pops another grape into his mouth, chewing. 'Who knows, the savages might attack.' He pauses, to let the words sink in. 'Who knows, he might not survive. Do you understand my meaning?'

A gleam comes to the young man's eye.

'I can return to Rome without Regulus.'

The old man reclines back, pleased.

'It would be better if you returned without him.' He sips wine from a silver cup. 'That would be ideal for our interests.'

'And riches?'

'Loot a temple. It should be easy.'

'All right. So be it. I'll do it.'

'Good, good. Now let us go and celebrate.' Cytheris the courtesan is having a soiree tonight. We can make the final deal with Regulus there.

Cytheris

I sit with my eyes closed, inhaling the scent of incense and sage leaves burning. Incense to chase the night spirits away. Sage to purify the air and help me focus. It is early. The Goddess came to me last night and as I sit quieting my mind, I try to feel Her for further instructions.

I am sat on the hardwood floor right next to my bed, the predawn light illuminating the frescoes on walls, chest of drawers and tumbled sheets. I slept alone last night. It was necessary so I can prepare for tonight's festivities. No affectionate lover, no warm body to disturb my rest. I woke up because my belly was warm with the memory of someone's hand on it. For just a moment I wasn't sure if I was alone, so I stretched slowly, like my cat Ginger, purring sounds, breasts up, head back, knees spread open, arms wide out reaching for air.

No one. Good. One must be careful with what names one whispers in the morning.

I get up quickly, open the window into the garden. The orange trees are filled with blossoms spreading their aroma. It's the smell of spring, of blood quickening; of bodies together in union. I pause and allow myself to drown in it, smiling. I make love to men and women every day of the year but this is my favourite season. The season of renewal and birth. The perfume of trees and flowers mixed with the smell of breath. The taste of strawberries mixed with the taste of sweat. Sweet and salty. Tart.

My maid is in the kitchen preparing breakfast – I hear her humming a high pitched tune.

Settling back into myself, back straight, legs firmly tucked, I focus on my breathing, like my teachers taught me many years ago.

'It is a gift, connecting with the Goddess, they said. 'Not many have it. You must honour it and obey her in everything she says. Even if you do not understand her reasons.'

I was thirteen when it started. My first blood came and went, consecrated in the usual ritual and festivities; everyone bowing as I sat wrapped in silk, adorned with garlands of flowers.

My teachers took the day off from their service to the goddess. The girls, the young ones looking on with envy, the elder ones smiling; the slaves, sombre – everyone lined up to give me morsels from dishes they prepared for me – rice with dates, raisins and pine nuts, pilaf wrapped in vine leaves, aubergines baked in the oven with herbs from our garden, bread – warm with butter and cheese melting, sticky in my mouth - creamy mushrooms with leeks and garlic, sticky honey cakes, apples crushed with spices. I ate and tasted from each hand what they had to offer to my new role as woman. Beer, wine, and music - the night was filled with dance and laughter.

The Goddess was gentle, she did not force herself, she hinted at places in my body I could explore with my fingers, each sensation new, making my cheeks burn in the morning.

For years she taught me the ways of pleasure – first, my own, then my friends, and finally, men.

Eros is power. Power to birth spirit into form. Power to create. Power to heal. Power to remove sorrow and suffering. Power to forgive.

It takes its toll on the body. So many want it, so many are hungry for it. They are forgetting how to honour my gift. It saddens me to see how rushed it is becoming, harsh. Some men can't even see me even though they are looking straight at me. I whisper 'I am yours, I am yours. We are here. You are good.' Some understand.

Minutes pass, I let go of these thoughts. Taking a deep breath, I connect with my essence, ground it into the earth. From here, notice how it's falling down into my pelvis, feel the rush of my womb opening down, down into the floor, the ground beneath it, I imagine the rocks layers, down into the hot lava core, rumbling untold power underneath the surface.

Another breath brings me back to the rhythms of my heart and this time I trace a line up into the ceiling, past the roof, up into the sky, past the moon, connecting to the sun and its radiant heat.

There's tingling in my arms. My legs feel heavy. My thoughts stop as I focus on heartbeat after heartbeat, feeling the blood rush in and out. One, two, three moments pass. I hear birds chirping. I hear my maid pouring water. I hear the cracking of the floor under me.

I see darkness and I feel the presence before I see it. A power, familiar, enveloping me. My spine straightens, belly filling my lungs with air.

She appears in a blaze of glory in front of my mind's eye. Glorious presence, impossible to describe. There are words mortals use. Power, light, strength, beauty, joy. None of these are enough. They fall short of what she is, like saying you are in love the first time you love. You write, you sing, you dance, you breathe love the first time you love. And still it's not enough to describe it. You only feel.

I observe her, in reverence and gratitude.

Follow the men.

'Which men? Where?'

Follow the men. She repeats and disappears. I open my eyes to the day. I am happy. I will see Regulus tonight. He understands.

Regulus

'Inadequate. Small and awkward. Like I've done something wrong. Like no matter what I do I cannot compare myself to you. That's how you make me feel, Regulus, and I hate you for it.' Lucrezia adjusts her golden necklace and smooths the skin on her face peering into her reflection. 'Oh, how I wish you were dead!' She says to herself.

There's a knock on the door before Regulus walks in carrying a tray.

'Why won't you have the slaves bring this?' She asks, appalled. 'You act like a peasant!'

'My dear wife,' he replies calmly. 'I am celebrating and could not allow anyone the arduous task of trying to get the wine you like just the way you like it so I did it myself.' He replies in a soothing tone.

He places the tray on the table by the settee that faces the doors opening into the garden. Slaves are sweeping the paths and planting fresh seeds. It's morning - the light, that pink colour only seen in the valleys outside Rome makes everything brighter. Crystal clear air, brisk, fresh - Regulus fills his lungs with its sweet smell before saying -

'I am leaving on a military expedition. With Titus Augustus. We are moving South then East.' He lets the words fall into the silence between them.

She turns to face him, sharply, face lighting up.

'What? When? How? How long will you be gone?' Questions rush, one after another. Too quickly.

'Can you at least try and pretend you are sad that I'm going away?' He sighs.

'Don't be ridiculous. This is great news. You will come back with new territory and wealth for the empire!' She walks up to him, gesturing. 'Finally you can rise in rank and I can wipe the smile off that she-wolf's face when..'

Regulus cuts her off with 'I might not come back.'

'What do you mean you won't come back? Of course you'll come back! No one is actually expecting you to fight the battles, are they? You've got soldiers who are paid to do that!'

Regulus inhales deeply, closing his eyes.

'I will not let my men die while I stand back idle, Lucrezia. You know me better than that.' His voice, firm, steely tone to it.

'I hate it when you get so stubborn. You're like a donkey, a mule that won't budge no matter how many times it's whipped.' She throws her arms out in frustration. 'Fine. Do whatever you want! If you want to leave me a widow, so be it.'

He turns to look at her. 'Sometimes I think that's exactly what you want, Lucrezia.' She opens her mouth in denial but closes it back – it's too late. The truth makes the air between them thick with sorrow.

'You are being absolutely ridiculous.' She mumbles walking off. 'We can celebrate this opportunity tonight. I must tell my father.'

Her footsteps echo off the marble floor. Regulus picks the glass of wine and drinks it in one gulp.

'Oh Zeus, does Hera hate you too?' He asks, facing the ceiling.

'Master.' A voice, a slave girl peers shyly at him.

'What is it?' He turns to look at her.

'A messenger has come, with a message to be delivered straight into your hand, master.' She pauses. 'You said to wait till you're alone to deliver messages from...'

Her voice trails off.

'Yes, yes. Send him in.' He circles to the settee and lowers himself in it.

A boy of twelve, tanned, all skin and bones walks up to him and hands him a folded and sealed letter.

'How is your mistress this morning?' Regulus asks.

'Communing with the goddess.' The boy answers.

'Does she want an immediate answer to this?'

'Yes.'

It's easy to break the seal. The paper is folded in four parts. He opens it and reads. His frown turns to a smile. Warmth in his voice as he replies, 'Tell your mistress my answer is always.'

The boy nods and runs off.

'Gallivanting with courtesans I see. Parting fuck before you leave?' Lucrezia walks back in, approaches her husband and takes the wine cup. 'To you, Regulus. May your mission be a success!' She gulps it down.

'Thank you.' Regulus doesn't react. 'More wine?'

'You won't go off to bring it yourself again, will you?'

'Not this time'. He gestures to the slave standing in the corridor. 'More wine please.' The man obeys immediately. Regulus turns back to his wife.

'Lucrezia, we need to talk.'

She sits down next to him.

'Indeed we do.' She replies, watching him expectantly.

'How old is our son now?' He asks.

She sits back, eyes narrowing. 'Twelve. Why?'

'It's time for him to learn how to be a man.'

'Over my dead body. You are not taking my son from me!' She sits up, pacing, voice rising. 'I don't know what you have in mind and I don't care. My son will stay by my side even if I have to chain him.' She pauses, pointing. 'Or you!'

'Lucrezia.'

'No.'

'You must understand that...'

'I said no.'

'Fine. Then he will grow up not knowing anything about how to be a leader of men. He won't know friendship. Or camaraderie. Or group effort. He won't know how to trust or build trust with his people.' Regulus pauses for breath, calming. 'Lucrezia, I am tired of arguing with you about this. Even you must see that he can't learn these things while he's at your side. There are skills he must know if he is to take responsibility for the family name.'

She is silent.

'Don't think I'm heartless. I understand your pain. It's hard for a mother to let go.'

She is silent.

'Lucrezia, please.' He pauses. Insists. 'Consider what is best for the family.' He leaves it at that.

'Where would you take him?' She asks, defeated.

'The same school I was trained in.'

'Wouldn't it be better if he went to father's school?'

'Let us consider and talk it over with him over dinner tonight. Will you invite your father too? This is an important decision that will influence the rest of his life.'

'I have already invited my father.' She answers, irritated. 'To celebrate with you the glorious expedition you're embarking upon.' She moves to leave.

Regulus goes back to watching the garden.

Before reaching the doorway, she turns around with hate in her eyes. 'I wish you would never come back,' she whispers.

'What did you say?'

'I'm sure my father will come here soon. He'll want to influence his grandson's life.'

'It started with Mars, the god of war, enchanted with Rhea the Vestal beauty. It started with two brothers, born of pain. What starts with cruelty carries cruelty forever.'

Letters

Chapter 3 Divine Union

Titus

The courtesan is dancing in front of me – she is beautiful. Brown skin reflects the fire from the torches on the walls, sweat gathered at her forehead and at the nape of her neck. A drop trickles down to her chin and falls to her chest, sliding down into her tunic. Her breasts pop up and down to the rhythm of her shaking, a tambourine marks her beat.

Regulus agreed to our mission. We are to ride south east in a week. This morning, one of my lieutenants appeared with news that Regulus is gathering loyal men, relatives to those he studied with at military school. This is good news. The more of his supporters we destroy, the better. I watch the woman swing her hips widely, belly shaking. I beckon for her to approach.

'Cytheris. Are you free tonight?'

'For you, I am always free my dear.' She answers coyly.

'Good. I am in the mood to celebrate.'

'Ah, I am honoured you have chosen me to celebrate with you! I'll go and make the necessary preparations. The usual?'

'Bring another with you. As I said, I am celebrating.'

'Yes, of course. Anyone specific you prefer?'

'A boy. Tall, slender, just beginning to break his voice. I saw him among your slaves.'

'Galep?' She pauses, unsure.

'Is he not in training with you?'

'Yes, but he has never...' She looks at her feet.

'A virgin? Oh. Even better! I am looking forward to this even more! What a gift, Cytheris! How much do you want for him?'

She doesn't answer.

'Cytheris?'

'Titus, I value your patronage highly, you know that.' She says, bowing her head. 'And I hope that the fact that you are here, celebrating in my company, is an indication that I please you with my services. As you said, the boy is in training and under my protection. It is better for his future ability to please if his first time is with someone gentle, someone kind to his needs.'

I don't like what she is implying. She notices.

'Do not misunderstand my meaning, please.' She says, hurriedly. 'I am certain it will be his honour to count you among his patrons once he develops the skills necessary to please you. May I offer an alternative? Another boy, only slightly older. The same slender frame. Has not changed his voice yet. He enjoys the same pleasures as yourself.'

'I want the virgin.'

'Titus.'

'Are you arguing with me, Cytheris?'

She sighs, about to give in.

'Cytheris! My apologies for being late, I had dinner with my father-in-law.'

Regulus walks in, red and breathing heavily. 'Titus.' He nods in my direction.

'Regulus.' I answer. 'Cytheris and I are in the middle of negotiating her services for this evening.'

He flushes a deeper red. He is too late and he knows it. The fat bastard.

'It was not my intention to interrupt you, Titus. I simply wanted to greet our gracious hostess this evening. This is her celebration after all.'

'Oh, is it? What are you celebrating, Cytheris?'

'The goddess spoke to me.'

'Did she, now? And what did she say?'

'She asked me to join your expedition.'

'The goddess asked you to join an army expedition as a common whore?' I can't help but laugh. 'She has a twisted sense of humour, that goddess of yours.'

'Titus, do not blaspheme against my goddess. She is not to be trifled with.'

'Whatever you say, Cytheris. Join us if you must. I'm sure my men will enjoy your company immensely.'

'I, for one, am looking forward to journeying with you, Cytheris.' Regulus bows in her direction.

'The pleasure will be all mine, I'm sure.'

'All right, all right, enough with the pleasantries.' I have to interfere. 'We were talking about your virgin boy, Cytheris. How much do you want for him?'

'Titus. He will not please you. He doesn't know how. Let me bring you someone who will.'

'Good to see you, Titus. Congratulations, Cytheris.' With that, Regulus bows off and leaves to get wine.

It's true. I require special attention. Attention that must be taught and explained in great detail. I have no time nor inclination to teach anyone now. But I want to experiment something new. I want the glow of youth on my skin. A tender, untouched mouth to bite and draw blood.

'Cytheris. I want the boy. Only him. I want him to be left alone with me. All night. Name your price. I will accept no argument or other offers.' I pause for effect,'If you value my family's patronage, that is.'

'Very well. Five thousand gold coins.'

It is too steep a price. Her house is worth half that. She knows it. I know it.

'Done. Bring him to me. Now.'

She walks off after the boy. I adore celebrating. I grab my goblet and join Regulus and the other patrons. They are watching three courtesans dance, dressed as the graces. The man in the middle holds an apple and they are competing for it.

'Oh Titus, I bet you'd compete for that morsel of a mortal, not the apple, they laugh.'

'He is not bad, but I prefer the sight of your sweet ass, senator Augustus.'

'Oh my tired old bones are no match for your vigour.' He giggles. 'Although, in my day.'

I come and kiss him, to the roaring laughter of the rest of the audience.

'You have some spunk yet, old man. That kiss was worthy of the most vigorous steed. In fact,' my hand slides to his groin, giving his balls a squeeze, 'I bet you can still give anyone the ride of their life.'

The group laughs uproariously as Cytheris approaches with the boy. He stands erect, not yet a man. His cheeks are red. He seems shy.

I am delighted. The short tunic covers his privates but not the lithe strong legs, the legs of a runner. His lips, so full, a faint trace of hair above them. Black hair and piercing blue eyes, sparkling with knowing. Ah, what a gorgeous parting gift!

'Titus, I'd like to introduce you to Galeb. He is most honoured to keep you company tonight.'

'Galeb, my master. I look forward to our fucking.'

The boy smiles, the beginning of pubescent hair above his lip making me moan inwardly.

'Ah, Titus, how fickle you are.' The senator moans. 'You leave me for the company of youth!' Dramatically, he raises his arm to his forehead. 'Alas, I am heartbroken.'

'My dear senator, I shall remember the taste of your kiss and pass it to the next generation.'

With that, I bow and turn my attention to Galeb. Take him by the hand.

'Come, let us go somewhere where we will be alone.'

I usher him to a room off the banquet hall. The room Cytheris usually reserves for me. She tries to follow us but I forbid it with a hand gesture.

It's sparsely furnished. A bed, a lamp, a torch on the wall. A wooden chest with oils and ointments. We won't need that.

The boy is trembling. I haven't decided yet what to do with him. Or how. I tell him to get undressed for inspiration. He obeys immediately. His member is small, that of a boy. Faint hair surrounds it.

'Do you touch yourself?'

'No, master.' The rush of being called a master washes over me. I have my answer.

'You are a clever boy. Keep calling me master and obey my every wish. Does your mistress whip you?'

'Sometimes, master.'

'Do you like it?'

'No master.'

'You must learn to like it with me. And you must ask for more. Understand?'

'Yes, master.'

'Turn around.'

He obeys.

'Bend over.'

He obeys.

'Spread your ass cheeks.'

He obeys.

'Have you washed yourself today?'

'Yes master.'

'Are you certain? Put your finger up there and check.'

He obeys.

'Lick your finger.'

He obeys.

'Are you clean?'

'No master.'

'Go clean yourself properly and bring a whip.'

He obeys, returning with Cytheris.

'What is the meaning of this?' I ask quietly.

'You asked for both of us, Titus, didn't you?'

'I changed my mind. Leave. Now.'

'But.'

'Leave.'

She throws one last look at the boy and goes out, closing the door behind her. He is trembling even harder. His hand shakes as he hands me the whip.

'Master. I only wish to please you.' He says.

I look at him. Young, face sad but his eyes, gleaming, sparkling. 'Your mistress angered me greatly. You will pay for it.' I state.

'Yes master.'

I unravel it, and whip him once. It falls on his chest and belly. He doubles over in pain, tears in his eyes.

'Ask me for more.'

'More, master.'

'Turn around.'

He obeys. I let it fall on his back this time, swift and biting. It draws blood.

'Ask me for more.'

'More master.'

This time it marks his shoulder. He screams and holds his arm over the wound. It pisses me off.

'Do not touch yourself. Only I am allowed to touch you. And I will tell you when you are to touch yourself. Understood?'

'Yes master.'

I whip him again. This time it marks his sweet ass.

'Do you understand?'

'Yes master.'

'Ask me for more.'

He is blubbering. He is crying in earnest now.

'More master.'

I've had enough.

'Bend over.'

He obeys.

'Spread your cheeks.'

He obeys.

'Ask me to fuck you.'

'Fuck me master.'

I plunge into him, once, twice, three times. He is tight and hot. He screams. I like it. I hold him by the hair and plunge deeper. I lick the blood off his back. Hold him by the hips. Jerking in and out. Hard. I can't control myself, I explode too quickly.

Breathing heavily I finally say. 'Turn around.'

He obeys. His face is streaked with tears and snot. I raise him by the chin and kiss his lips. Slowly. Exquisitely. The kiss the ladies dream of. So tender. I push my tongue into his mouth. He answers with a flicker of his. His member is erect against my thigh. I know exactly how to please little boys. He jerks, spreading his semen all over my face as soon as my lips hold him in my mouth. Messy little boy. I wipe it off with my hand. Kiss him again.

'Now you know what to do.'

I push his head down. He takes me in.

'No teeth. That's right. Use your tongue on the tip. That's right. Let me go deep into your throat. That's right.'

I grab his head and push it up and down.

'You're such a good slave. You know exactly how to please your master. Good slave. Don't speak. Keep sucking. Don't stop. Like that.'

I excel at slave training. If I do say so myself.

'Power over others. It's not possible without agreement. But to break from its chains, first, we face the shadow in ourselves.'

Letters

Rania

The lowest terrace in front of the temple is decorated with flower garlands and vines. Slabs of graphite are warming in the pits. Meat sizzles there. Baskets of berries and nuts are arranged in a circle around the fire, where fish and game bakes under hot coals. Someone is playing the flute. It's the shepherd, a young boy. He must be Aanaka and Sia's age. He is holding their attention with his tune; they sit, listening.

We guided Leena through her ceremony in the inner sanctum of the temple this morning. She had been sitting at the feet of the Goddess the rest of the day, receiving offerings from visitors trailing up the steep hill, laden with packages, woven baskets filled with fruit, sacks of grain, sheepskins with oil or wine, chests with precious myrrh. Everyone celebrating her initiation. A new priestess. A new healer. One they could be proud to tell their grandchildren about.

'How much longer do you think he can hold their attention?' Mina asks me, looking in the direction of the shepherd boy.

'Oh, I'd say about ten, nine, eight, seven...'

Sia is the first to look around. She notices us. Blushes and gets up quickly and with a, 'this is a stupid song,' runs off.

'Wait, where are you going?' Aanaka jumps and hurries to join her.

The boy stops, the flute giving one last high note. He looks at us laughing and walks off to sulk.

'How is she doing?' I ask. I have been overseeing the cooking and the eating, having a few morsels myself.

'Who, Leena? Very well. Doesn't let her tiredness show at all. Greets everyone with a smile and is very grateful for each gift.' Replies Mina looking at the temple, illuminated by the afternoon sun.

'We did well, didn't we?' I ask.

'Yes. You can be proud of your daughter.'

'My sister now. She is a priestess today.'

'Whatever you want to call her. I don't know why you insist on denying your blood ties.'

'I want her to be independent and free. My duty as mother is done now. She is grown up.'

'She still needs her mother. You are too hard on her.'

'Has she complained?'

'You know she won't complain. You taught her not to.'

'Exactly. Our new sister is patient, kind, and wise beyond her years. Skilled at maintaining life but not afraid of death. I have done my duty as a mother. Oh go on, let us celebrate! Wine?'

'Not yet. I have to check on a few more things at the temple but I'll be back.'

Mina walks off leaving me perplexed. Does Leena still need to be mothered? I thought I was done with the needy ties of children.

I make my way into the hall where she sits, surrounded by offerings. The light falls on her face. Her eyes are closed. She opens them and lights up with tenderness and pride.

'Rania. You're here.'

'Of course. I am so proud of you, my dear. You are already a gifted healer. I am honoured to have you among my sisters.' I say kindly.

Her face falls. I feel her pain at being rejected. Being my sister means not being my charge any longer. Being my sister means responsibility. Being my sister means she can no longer call me mother. She still wants to be my daughter.

'Come, let us go for a walk. I would like to show you something.' I say to cheer her up.

She sits up and walks up to me. I hug her close, enveloping her in my love, embracing her fully. She presses against me, tight. She is my gift. I have sheltered, nourished, and protected her all her life. I have shown her my way and transmitted all my learning through words and deeds and exchanges at levels beyond physical understanding. It's time for me to stand back and let her try her wings and continue with her own journey. But these are not things you can say in words. I break our embrace and guide her to the exit. We walk out, leaving a trail of flower petals behind.

I take her to the orchard terrace where apple trees share space with pears, apricots, and cherries. Ancient stone slabs rest in a circle in the centre of a clearing.

'My dear, do you know the story of these stones?'

'No, Rania.'

'When the temple was founded, these stones were already here, carrying inscriptions in a language we did not understand. A few generations of priestesses spent considerable time copying the message and carrying it with them on their travels, hoping to find someone who could read and translate its meaning. It took many years of travel but one of them finally ran into an ancient crone who could read and translate them for us.'

I pause, letting my fingertips slide over the carvings on the slab. Leena sits on the grass, leaning her back against the stone, tucking in her legs.

'Do you want to know its meaning?' I ask finally.

'Yes, please.'

'You know I did not grow up in this temple, like you did. Marwa brought me here. First in the spirit realm and then physically. She travelled to my native land and reached an agreement with the elders who raised me to initiate me into this sisterhood as part of my journey into separation.'

'Separation?'

'Yes. It has been agreed to cede power to men, temporarily, so, we, as a collective, learn the lessons inherent in power over others. The sacred connection we hold and are with all that is will be forgotten.'

'Why?'

'The collective is ready to play the game of duality.'

'More than now?'

'We choose to go deeper, yes.'

'What does this have to do with the inscription?'

'I was coming to that. Be patient,' I continue. 'I moved into the temple and it was during the spring equinox that I found a parchment in the library with the words that made me shiver when I read them. I asked Mina at the time where they came from and she brought me to these stones.'

'What did the inscription say?'

I ease my way down to sit in front of her. I remember the words by heart. Looking deep into her eyes, I want to transmit what I felt and what it meant for me, not just the sounds. I take a deep breath and sit in silence for a while, letting the moment build.

A younger voice, still mine, speaks the words I read out loud many years ago.

'For those who seek divine union, know this. All is you. There is nothing in the heavens or on earth that is not you. The gods are your eyes in the realms of spirit and the trees are your eyes in the realm of flesh. Every blade of grass knows your name. Every bird sings your song. You are divine. When the divine comes together with itself, the heavens and the earth merge to create a new universe. That is the meaning of procreation.'

In silence she comes to me for another embrace. I cuddle her close, the way I used to when she was little.

'You were conceived here in divine union, my precious. I am honoured to be your mother.'

'And now your sister.'

'Yes.'

'I love you.'

'I love you too.'

Chapter 4 To love and to hold

The Goddess

The crow cries us all to attention. Leena freezes, listening. Diana, our seer, slumps to the floor, the front temple column supporting her back.

'It has begun,' She whispers, looking into the distance. 'We must hold love or we will be destroyed. Do not allow fear to overcome you. Hold love for yourselves and for them.'

'Who is coming, Diana?'

'The new men. The warriors. Three days.'

'How many?'

'One hundred and fifty.'

We ready ourselves. Bathe. Prepare lodging should they want to stay. Make sure we have enough to feed them.

Aanaka is skipping between the rose bushes when she sees them.

'They are here, they are here!' She shouts out.

We all come out to greet the new men. They are to be our allies. Together we will forge the new world – a world where we teach them about power.

There we stand, all thirteen of us – connected by love welcoming them, wanting to love them.

Their intentions are not as pure.

They do not see us as teachers. Or healers. They do not want to learn anything.

What they want is to surround us, walking up the hill, slowly.

Leena walks to greet them, slowly, holding out a flower to their leader. He looks at her, smirks and with a gesture, swift and practised, cuts off her arm.

'No!'

Aanaka, followed by Deena, ran to stop them. Leena is shouting, 'Rania, Rania, I'm bleeding.' Mina is shouting, 'We must hold love for them,' holding on to Sia, who is jerking, trying to escape, screaming 'Aanaka'. Bianca is breathing deeply, tears streaming down her face, whispering, 'We love you, we love you.'

A soldier, small and stocky, dark haired and handsome hacks Deena with a blade, cutting her little body. Aanaka, kicking and screaming, beats one of them with her fists, not really slowing him down. He shakes her off. She falls. The next soldier steps on her leg and pierces her throat with his sword.

I scream, we all scream.

'Enough! Stop this madness!'

They keep on advancing.

We hide in the temple. Bar and lock the doors against the intruders. Stand at the entrance, looking at each other, too shocked to absorb what has happened. Mina recovers first.

'Our love must become fierce now.' She faces us, with her back to the doors that are pummelled and pounded by a log from outside, the soldiers trying to get in. Her eyes blaze with contained fury as she staccatos every word, her voice booming in the cavernous hall.

'They are not asking for permission to enter. They are using a tree to force their way into our temple and our lives. They have killed three of our girls. They do not intend to learn from us. They want our power. Let us show them that they cannot hold it. Be full of power now. Connect to the Goddess' full nature, her fierce love. That which protects all creation.' She stands, feet wide apart, grounding herself into the temple, the earth itself, down to its core. Her body relaxes into the moment. We take the same stance, connect to the same steaming heat, slow and merciless in its path.

'I call on our lineage.' She begins, her voice not coloured by emotion. 'I call on our mothers, grandmothers, and priestesses that came before, serving the balance.' She lets the words fall and form a circle around ours. 'I call on all aspects of the same goddess, in all lands, in all times.'

The sound of the soldiers pounding our door outside dims. She pronounces every name, pausing for a breath in between. She looks at each of us as she names the goddess that is closest to our homeland, the one we heard of since childhood. The name that has been guiding us all our lives up to this point. A connection intimately known and felt.

'Kali.' She looks at Nimra and Saadia with a smile. They smile back, relaxing, starting to undulate with the power raising up their spine.

'Sekhmet.' Aat, Dedeyet, and Berenib exchange glances and start stretching and moving their bodies to the sound of the drum that Sai started playing, marking a rhythm, gathering like thunder.

'Durga.' Diana walks over to Mina and places a hand on her shoulder. I can feel her accessing her power and amplifying it into the room, into all of us.

'Ereshkigal.' Bianca crouches on the floor, hands spread wide. She joins her energy to ours.

'Inanna.' Mina says as Marwa begins a dance around our circle, making sounds with her throat, the sounds of a storm beginning in the distance, approaching closer.

'Ishtar.' Mina draws out the vowel, the name feels like a snake, hissing. We come closer to each other, completing the circle, joining hands. We stand still.

Mina looks at me. 'Lillith.' She names the final goddess, tongue out between her teeth. She holds it there, ending the sound, sending the primordial energy.

We take a breath in unison. Release it, slowly. Step back. Turn around, our backs to each other. Our girls and Marwa in the middle of our circle.

The drumming stops. The pounding on the door stops. The air is thick with power. We are filled to the brim with the force that created the universe. It calmly retreats, like waters from shore before a tsunami, building momentum. There is no need for words. We are ready to destroy and be destroyed.

They burst through, with screams of valour. We respond by moving swiftly, robbing them of their knives, slicing their throats. Our screams of rage pierce the silence, every hit and punch is loaded with so much energy the air cracks, skulls cracks against our pestles, men fall to the ground moaning in pain pressing against their torn arms and broken bones. Time ceases to exist. The more blood we see, the more it feeds our lust for more. We scream blood curdling growls of women, annihilating everything in their path. We use the steel of their dead to cut and gash and fill our worship hall with blood. Blood that we are not afraid of. Blood that we use to strengthen us. Blood that is as familiar to us as the sound of laughter. We bathe in theirs.

Titus

I lie on the floor of the temple, watching my men die. These sorceresses are more powerful than I expected. Clearly, twenty soldiers aren't enough to defeat them. We need reinforcements.

'Retreat!' I shout over the sounds of the battle, getting up.

'Retreat.' The few surviving men echo, heading for the exit.

As soon as we give up the fight, the women stop attacking. They look around at each other and then at the men leaving the temple past me, standing in the doorway.

'Don't come back.' One of them says, looking at me. I hold her gaze. She understands that I will. She turns away.

I pause surveying the scene. My men lie on the floor, some dead with arms torn, throats open, some still moving. One of the women approaches a soldier, he is dragging himself towards me slowly, his back to her. She crouches over him and plunges a short sword into his neck, severing the vertebrae. He dies immediately. Taking no prisoners, I see.

'Rania, what are you doing?' One of the priestesses asks.

'I will not heal these men. They are suffering. I am ending it.'

She goes after the next one.

The other women start attending to the dead, dragging them into a pile in the corner. The girls are quietly sitting against the columns, looking into the distance with wide eyes. One of them gets up to help carry the bodies. The others follow suit.

'Call Daniel.' Rania says to one of them. 'Tell him to bring a wheelbarrow.'

No one is paying attention to me.

I look at the altar, the pedestal and statue of the goddess is pure gold. She is frozen in a dance, her eyes are made of rubies the size of my fists and her crown is studded with diamonds the size of a human eye. She's wearing a necklace of emeralds and her belly button is a sapphire. Golden bracelets and anklets decorate her arms and legs. There's a pouch of gold coin at her feet as an offering next to bowls with flower petals. The burning incense covers the smell of blood. The tapestries covering the walls are spun in silk, their colours bright. Delicate porcelain vases now streaked with blood stand between the columns and against the walls, covered with gold motifs. The ceiling is pure gold. I want to see their coffers. I wonder if they have any slaves at this temple that can be sold in the markets. Melting the statue alone will be enough to fund another expedition further into the wild forests of the North. Regulus is wrong. The goddess did not strike me. She is rewarding me with her bounty. It's a good day.

I count the women left standing. There are seven. They look shocked and tired. Three girls.

I turn to leave but the priestess, done with killing every other man in the room, catches my eye before I turn away. I don't know what she sees. I don't care.

'They will be back.' She says to the others.

'I know.' I hear as I walk away.

I reach the foot of the hill. The sun is shining and a lark begins a song. We found gold, rubies, diamonds, and silks. We found women and girls. I am looking forward to this. The men are sitting by their tents, some in a circle, some are brushing their horses. They stand at my approach.

'Titus, what are your orders?' I look at the five men that retreated with me. They are subdued. Their pride is hurt. They did not expect to be so defeated. What they saw in that temple had scared them, reminded them of childhood terrors and old wives tales of female demons feeding on blood. The power of the gods was in that temple and they sensed it. Religious superstition will cloud their minds and make them weak. I need them to go back in there and fight. Fortunately, I know a way to make a goddess mortal.

'Men, how long has it been since you were with a woman?'

Some smile, some mumble.

'Since this morning, I'm always ready for more.' One shouts. The rest explode with laughter.

'Good. Now, there are seven women and three girls left in that temple. They have killed fifteen of your comrades, mercilessly slicing their throats and tearing their limbs. These men were your friends. They had wives who are now widows because of these women.'

'Aye, they had the goddess on their side.' I hear.

'You are right. They worship an ancient goddess. I have seen her altar and her statue. She is made of pure gold, rubies, and diamonds. She is not Venus, Minerva or Vesta. She is not Bellona. She is some barbarian fury who has no power.'

'We had to retreat. That is enough power for me.'

'I too am saddened at the death of our men. It shows that we were not prepared. But we know better now. We know what they are capable of, don't we?'

They nod.

'I have surveyed them. There are only seven left. They are in shock and tired. Look around you. How many men can you count?'

'One hundred.'

'That's right. One hundred brave Roman soldiers, trained in battle. I ask you now, men. What will we do with these women?'

'Kill them!' They shout. More men approach us.

'Don't you know your friends' children will be forced into slavery to pay their father's debts? Don't you know these women have taken the lives of brave men who fought side by side with you in many battles?'

'Are you going to let them have an easy death?'

'No!' Roaring.

'We are Romans! Our king is counting on us. Mars is with us. Show them what we do to barbarians! Show them what we do to those who take one of ours!'

One hundred and thirty men ran up the hill into the shadows of the temple hall. I follow slowly, listening for screams.

They come, inevitably. Then laughter. Grunts. My men were inventive in games of torture. Once their lust was satisfied, they played with the bodies, plunging swords into the women to make them jerk at the exact moment of climax. I'd seen it all before.

Regulus approaches me as I stand outside watching the sun set on the valley.

'What have you done, Titus?'

'Secure wealth for our king, commander.'

'This is not honourable.'

'There is no honour in war.'

'There is honour in serving the kingdom. There is honour in defending our home. This is not war. This is slaughter.' He falls silent for a few moments. Then continues. 'The gods will punish us for this sacrilege.'

'We will see.'

I had to interfere once I heard the vases breaking. Entering the temple hall, filled with my men, laughing and shouting.

'Ho!' I yell so they all hear their commander's voice. One by one they stop what they're doing and fall silent. I survey them one by one. 'Romans, you've done well. You've defeated the enemy. Glory to Rome!'

'Glory to Rome!' They shout in unison.

'Look around you.' I continue 'This is a rich temple. Mars is rewarding us for our bravery. See the goddess?' I point to the altar, 'She is silent.'

I pause to let it sink in.

'Sergeants, find all the slaves and bring them outside. The rest of you, carry the tapestries and all the valuables you can find back to camp. Tonight, we feast a great victory!'

Shouts of mirth fill the temple walls as men drop the bodies of women and girls onto the floor and disperse into the halls. One of them gives a last kick to the priestess that was killing my wounded men earlier. She breathes in, still alive. I leave her. She won't be alive for long.

Karma

Do you want me to continue this story?

Yes.

All stories start with a yes, you see - the heroine is asked, clearly, at the very beginning, if she will accept a step.

Yes, she will say and so the story begins, taking her down a winding path, always unexpected. Not always fun, unless you look at the really, really big picture. Then you become such a drunken lunatic that everything is funny. Especially death.

After the garrison of Roman soldiers took over the temple of the goddess they destroyed the altars, burned the orchard and the sacred grove.

After they murdered all the girls that were in our care.

After that, they raped us. We kicked and bit and scratched and drew blood.

They held us down and hit us. They punched our bellies and kicked our noses in and threw us against the walls so hard we lost consciousness.

They then tore our clothes, spread our thighs apart and raped us one by one.

Over a hundred of them.

This was no fertility ritual. This was no divine union of the masculine and the feminine. This was insanity.

They brutalised my body. I who could sense other's pain so clearly found my own being amplified by what my sisters suffered. My heart stopped, I was ready to leave until one of them decided to give me one last kick into the stomach, causing my lungs to inhale one more breath.

With it, the healer in me burst forth into a new identity, that of Lilith. She turned into me.

Who am I?

I am Karma, the soulless.

'In the space between thoughts is where you first identify who you are. Start with noticing the silence. As the sound of your breath brings you into the present moment, expand the silence to include everything.'

Letters

.

Rania was in shock. Everything she held true about the world was annihilated with a violence she couldn't comprehend. While she froze, trying to adjust to this new reality, I took over with one imperative - survive. I closed my eyes and focused on breathing as slowly as possible, while the soldiers ransacked our home, taking everything they could get their hands on. The dull thud of the goddess' statue being torn down made the temple floor and everyone on it tremble.

The shouts 'this way', soldiers going into the inner sanctum where we performed the most sacred rites. Bursting through the doors to the rooms, I heard Daniel's feeble 'no' before the sound of steel let me know he was gone. Another wave of loss shudders through Rania. I won't let her weep, the dead don't weep.

A soul doesn't just leave human consciousness, you see. It takes time and pain.

I do not move until the sound of their sandals die in the distance. Slowly, I raise myself on all fours and move to the nearest column. Sit against it, surveying the scene, allowing my eyes to adjust to the darkness. The bodies of my sisters lie there, darker shadows against the grey background. I strain my ears to hear. No footsteps. Good.

I get up, supporting myself on the column and walk towards the light that is the gate to the great hall. The door, broken in, is cracked, splintered. I run my fingers on the jagged edges. The beauty of the carving interrupted, its inner fibres exposed. What was whole is now ripped apart.

There is no moon. I stand at the temple gates. The trees that used to give us shade are smouldering. They did not touch the lower terraces. There's the river and on its banks, fires are burning, shadows moving on the tents pitched around them. The wind carries laughter and music. Closer, crickets are singing. No footsteps. Good.

I turn away and walk towards the back of the temple, to our water spring. It's a small spring, the water coming from the depth of the mountain into a pool of white marble decorated with mosaic. I sit on the edge for a while. They didn't take the ceramic jug. I fill it and pour water over my body, letting the ground soak the blood. The cold releases the shock enough to let me move with more energy. I throw away the torn tunic, pour jug after jug over me. Drink some. Pour some more. Finally, I get into the pool, immersing myself fully, take a deep breath and let my head go under. Outside sounds disappear and I listen to my heartbeat.

I wash away all traces of blood. It takes longer to wash away the semen. It's stuck to my skin. Anger rushes through me. No. Not yet. Clean. Rub. Scrub.

Finally, when I run my hands up and down my body, my fingertips only perceive the texture of my own skin, I come out of the pool.

I limp to the back entrance leading to the dispensary. I open the door. The hinges are well oiled, so it makes no sound. I pause to listen.

No footsteps.

Good.

Supporting myself on the walls, I almost fall over Daniel's body in the corridor. Drag him into a room to my left and take another tunic from the chest inside. Walk further down the corridor to the door of the dispensary. They did not burn it and had not taken any medicines. I know this room like I know my own body. The room has no windows; it's safe to have some light. I find a flint and light a lamp. Look around at the shelves of bottles, vials, boxes of balms and creams, linen pouches with dried herbs, embroidered with their names.

This, I know how to do.

Heal.

I pour some rosewater onto a linen bandage cloth and gently rub my face, pausing at open wounds. Neck, shoulders, chest. Arms, wrist to elbow, elbow to shoulder. Left leg, toes to ankle, ankle to knee, knee to thigh. Right leg. I cover my whole belly with the soaked fabric, placing my hands on the lower of my abdomen, where my womb is throbbing with pain and pure rage, feeling.

Spreading warmth.

Spreading.

I clean my wounds with a tincture that makes the skin tingle, slowly, deliberately, as gently as I can. Gulp a strengthening tonic. Pour some more rosewater and place the bandage between my legs.

It hurts.

No, Rania, we can't weep now.

Not yet.

I light my way down to the cellar, find a bottle of wine. The memory of Daniel handing it to Mina as a gift flashes before my eyes as I open it. Take a deep swig. Feel the warmth engulf my pain, dull the need for tears. Another swig. I don't notice the delicate flavours, only the relief.

I walk back out to the temple hall, where the bodies of my sisters lie. Pause at the entrance. Close my eyes but they are imprinted, they don't disappear. Drink some more.

Rania needs to grieve.

I approach Diana first. She's lying with her arm over her eyes, as if asleep. Down on my knees, I move her arm to reveal her face. Kiss her lips. I drag her to the centre of the hall, laying her on the side. One by one I find my sisters, kiss them, drag them, make a circle of their bodies, head resting on feet. Mina, the keeper of the coin. Bianca, Arina, and Livia, the lovers. Berenib, Nimra, and Saadia, traders, travellers, gatherers of knowledge. Aat, Dedeyet, and Shamal, the teachers. Marwa, the shaman. Dead.

No, Rania, not yet. Soon.

Now, the girls. Sai, the mathematician, the drummer, I lay in front of her guardian, Mina. Sonia, the storyteller, in front of her guardian, the seer Diana. Baby Ruth, pure love embodied, I hold for a while. I bury my face in her curls. How can I let go?

I sob, it escapes me.

I lay her down gently and get up to find the bottle of wine. Gulp, gulp to drown the wave of grief threatening to overtake me.

Not fucking yet.

Breath after breath pushes the pain down. I recover control. I walk outside into the cool air, looking for my apprentice, my daughter, my Leena in the darkness. She's lying in a heap, on the path the soldiers had taken, one arm cut off, still seeping blood. I check her breath. She's gone.

I take her to the pool, placing her dismembered arm on her belly while I carry her.

Rania's shock threatens again, like madness. I can't let her, not yet. Not yet.

I clean what's left of her arm. Tear off a strip from my tunic and bind her hand back to her body.

It won't heal, I know.

Take her to the great hall, place her inside the nest made up of parts of me.

Quickly, go back out for Aanaka, the builder and Deena, future lover. What future?

I am strong enough to carry them both in. I lay them with the others. Sit in the middle.

I leave the bottle of wine outside.

Rania

Rania cuddled Leena all night, rocking back and forth. Holding her close, feeling the warmth leave her body. Wailing. Trying to cover up the hole in her belly. Like a gash it opened, pouring out pain, stabbing pain. Pain that caught the breath of life and turned it into death. Turned it into sobs that caught in her throat. Sounds of raw agony that came from a place she never knew existed. No words. She could not speak.

It did not subside with the next breath. It grew worse with the next breath. The next breath brought the realisation that she was lying on the temple floor, in front of the altar, surrounded by her sisters and her children. Bodies slowly stiffening.

There was no understanding of this. Who can ever understand the loss of love and family? How is it possible to reach a level of acceptance of a fact that is happening to you? Yes, you, who only this morning kissed this brow, caressed this cheek, and held this hand.

This was some nightmare that she would wake up from, eventually. Yet, no matter how hard she pinched herself awake, they were there, growing colder and colder in the night.

On and on she wailed, her eyes going from one sister to the next, from one little girl to another. No traces of them left.

She did not feel them anymore.

Empty now, silent they were.

It felt like the tearing apart of the very fibres of her being, this silence. It felt like the sky was falling and the ground would swallow her up and she would be torn into a million pieces and be churned and made one with the earth and stone. It felt like dying.

She could join all of them. It was simple. All she had to do was drink from any of the poison vials. She had so many options. She could choose to go peacefully, sleep like this, among them. Wake up a babe again, in another life. Forget.

Slowly, she laid Leena next to Ruth deciding to go back to the dispensary for the vial. First on her knees, falling head first into Marwa's belly, weeping.

'Give me strength,' she whispered and stood up, teetering, going from one column to the next, stopping to let the waves of grief wash over her in an endless thought of -

Why am I still alive?

Why am I still alive?

Why am I still alive?

Stumbling and falling, holding on and letting go, she reached the dispensary where the light still illuminated neat rows of vials and herbs. The poisons were in an iron wrought plain chest with no inscription and a padlock. The key was inside one of the amulets hanging from her neck. She opened the lid, gingerly touching each vial. There were three.

The one on the left, a dark brown colour, she knew, would make her foam at the mouth and her muscles to spasm, stopping the heart and lungs.

The one in the middle would cause her to sleep and never wake up. It was the gentlest poison she had, for patients that suffered too much and needed to go in peace.

The one on the right would make her sick for days on end, slowly wasting away into oblivion.

Putting all three vials into a pouch at her waist, she walks back to the worship hall, approaches the circle of women and sits in front of them, legs crossed.

'I will soon be with you,' she whispers, taking out the glass bottles and uncorking them one by one.

She places them on the floor in front of her. She doesn't know which is which – it's hard to tell in the darkness.

Looking up at the altar, she addresses the empty space where the statue used to be.

'Before I go, I want some questions answered, oh goddess of life and death.' She continues, pausing after each question, no catch in her voice, steely, determined.

'Number one. Why was love not enough?'

'Number two. Who are these new men?'

'Number three. Why am I still alive?'

Silence was her answer.

She screams, forgetting all danger.

'Answer me!'

Silence.

Even the gods don't interfere with the choice of life or death. They understand how hard it is to breathe sometimes. Or face another dawn.

She lies down facing the ceiling, picturing leaving her body; merging with the light of all existence. No more suffering. No more pain. No more choices to make. Reunited with her sisters. Coming back for another life, a simpler life perhaps. An easier life. One of a peasant. A tradesman. A rich heir to a family fortune, cuddled and loved. A princess, spoiled with care and showered with gifts and poems.

Anyone but this. Anyone but Rania.

Turning on her side, she moves her gaze from the opened vials to the pile of bodies that were the meaning of her life.

Hours pass.

Grey dawn softens the dark corners of the hall and the shadows retreat.

She sits up and puts the corks back on the vials and gathers them back into the pouch on her waist.

'I'll do it tomorrow.' She says to the altar. 'You have not answered my questions.'

Walking outside, numb from lying motionless on the floor, she goes into the shed and takes out wood and starts building a funeral pyre at the entrance to the temple. It would be a sacrilege but these walls have already been defiled. No one will serve here again. The fire will cleanse the horror and with the smoke, erase all traces of her past. She hopes it will remove them from her memory too.

Log after log fit neatly to form a square large enough to fit all the bodies. After the final piece of wood is laid in place, she goes into the dispensary and brings out all the medicines, potions, creams, herbs and oils – it takes several trips. Focusing on these tasks numbs the pain for a while. Eases her mind enough to think and plan for the future. She chooses the essentials for healing and strengthening her body, pushes them into a sack and throws the rest onto the pyre.

The task of dragging the bodies onto the wood pile is not easy; they are heavier and much more rigid than when alive. When it's finally done, she goes into the garden and cuts off twelve roses and six daisies to place on each chest. Roses for her sisters, daisies for her children.

No weeping this time.

She is aware that she is hungry. Going back into the empty kitchens, she cuts out bread and cheese and chews, swallowing, gulping down water from a jug on the table. She finds goat milk and drinks that too. Pausing at the entrance on the way back for a moment.

In her room there's a chest of clothes – tunics, dresses, and wraps that she gathered over the years. The tunic for funerals is made of undyed silk but she leaves it in the trunk.

Instead, she chooses a woollen red dress – one worn during the most sacred rituals – and sets it aside to change into.

In the corner, there's a clay basin with water in it. She washes her face and neck, her arms and forearms, using a linen towel to dry off.

She walks to her bed and sits, surveying the room, trying to find a word for her feelings, finding none.

She lies down for a moment, curls up. Closes her eyes. Falls asleep.

Chapter 5 Loot

Regulus

I watch the men chew meat they tear off skewers. They drink wine straight from bottles, swinging, clinking them in celebration. Some are examining delicate golden necklaces that they took from the temple, some wear golden crowns on their heads, dancing to the tune of a lute someone is playing. Some are sitting quietly, staring into the fire, drinking themselves into oblivion. I am not the only one who tastes the bitterness of this victory.

Titus is sitting in the middle of a group of his men. They are replaying scenes from the massacre, gesturing at how they defeated their enemy. They go quiet at my approach, whispering and snickering behind my back.

'Commander,' Titus says. 'Please, join us. We were just talking about our brave battle of today. You have a way with words. We should compose a ballad that the bards can sing far and wide. Let all the temples everywhere fear us. The goddess is dead.'

'Aye, aye,' his men shout, drinking.

It takes all my self-control to keep my tone even.

'This is no great victory. These were women and children not trained in battle. A ballad would shame the name of our king.'

I look at him, arrogant and drunk. 'We leave at dawn. Have the men ready.'

I walk over to my tent and find Cytheris sitting up at my entrance.

'What are you doing here? I am not in the mood.'

'What troubles you?' She asks, standing a few paces away.

'Nothing.' I go towards the trunk in the corner. 'I've got letters to write.'

'I know a great song to soothe a troubled mind. Let me play it for you, as a gift.'

You don't refuse a woman's gifts.

'Fine,' I say, going over to the bale of straw that serves as my bed, lying down. 'Let's hear it.'

She brings out a cithara, sits down on the edge and starts plucking at the strings. A tune that begins like a spring rivulet running down the mountain, slowing down to a more sombre rhythm, rising and lowering in octaves. In a deep, velvety voice she repeats the words over and over again, changing the pitch and tone from forceful to calm, to yielding.

'*Men offer their deeds to gods -*

And -

Gods laugh at the deeds of men.'

The last time, she sings smiling, the warmth of it in her voice. I can't help but smile too.

'Come here, Cytheris. You've pleased me.' I say.

She leaves the instrument aside and crawls over to me, slowly.

'Is your mind calmer now?' She asks, snuggling beside me. Supporting herself with a raised arm.

'Yes. Thank you.' I look at her face. Her brown skin is soft, with black freckles on her nose. Her eyes, large and almond-shaped are framed by lashes dark as the night. They are moist and sparkle with humour and understanding. Feeling her body next to mine makes me tingle. She caresses my face and the back of my spine awakens, uncoiling rising up to my heart, to my eyes and into hers.

I caress her skin, slipping her tunic off her shoulder, looking at the shape of her breast, the nipple dark. She smells of spices and wine. Her tongue is sweet, flickering in and out of my mouth. I pull away and kiss her neck and shoulder, tracing a path down her arm to the palm of her hands, pausing at her wrist, feeling her pulse.

I clasp her hand, fingers interlacing and move it to my chest so she can feel my heartbeat. She taught me her ways the first night we spent together – I don't fear I won't please her. I know she will please me.

In her, with her, being present here, I forget the horrors of the day. They wash off of me like sweat droplets under a waterfall.

We fall asleep in each other's arms. She leaves in the middle of the night. Too soon it's time to wake up.

'Men loved women with their whole essence. The strength of one did not diminish the other's. And we spoiled them rotten. The juiciest fruit, the prettiest stones, the shiniest trinkets, if they liked them – we carried and placed them at their feet because who else are you going to love with all your heart?

What other being in this world can hold, and soothe, and love you back more?'

Letters

Karma

The person who woke up that evening had no memory.

She looks around the room for clues. She sees the darkened window, a table laden with jars and pots, and a full length mirror. She raises her hand in front of her face looking at the ridges and lines on her palms. Rubs them together. Her body is sore and bruised, it hurts to sit up. She feels nothing. No fear, no worry, no anticipation. She walks to the mirror to take a look at herself.

It distorts her face slightly but she can clearly see her blue eyes. One of them is swollen. A gash on her temple opened and blood seeped out while she slept, caked now. She touches her nose gingerly and winces at the sharp pain.

Someone gave me quite a beating.

She takes off her tunic and stands naked, surprised at all the bruises on her ribs and thighs, marks from fingers and tiny cuts on her skin.

I need a bath.

Somehow she knows where it is. She walks outside to the water well and sinks into the fountain, gently roaming her hands along her body so that the water undulates against it. She plays with her hair, spreading it out and down, massages her scalp, drops down to the bottom, listening to the silence. Her heart is thumping loud as if panicked but she doesn't register any emotion at all.

She comes up for air, her dark hair falling past her shoulders down to her waist.

Time to get dressed for the ceremony.

She stands up, squeezes her hair and stretches. Walks back to the room with the mirror, leaving wet footprints on marble floors in her wake.

Pats herself dry with a cloth, walks over to the table and opens one of the jars. The oil inside smells nice. She rubs it into her skin, starting with her left leg, her thigh, her belly, her arms and neck and breasts. She warms some more in the palm of her hands and massages her face. Cups her hand and pours more, spreads it loosely on her palm and untangles her hair, running oily fingers through the strands. She weaves a loose braid that falls heavy down to her thighs. Looking around the room for something to wear she notices the red tunic laid out on the chest. Walking over and picking it up, she holds it up to the light. It's thin and light, woven in wavy patterns with embroidered trees, animals, and flowers in silk thread. She puts it on and walks back to the mirror to adjust herself. It fits her well, accentuating her shoulders and neck, the fabric draping against her curves all the way to the floor. There is a small jar with a brush next to it on the table by the mirror that she opens, pausing, looking at herself.

What was the paint for? Ah yes, rage.

Like a key, this word unlocks her mind and she remembers the horror of last night, her life destroyed by soldiers wielding short swords, invading their space with cruelty and murder. In pain she looks into her own eyes, holds her own gaze, unflinching. Someone else looks through those eyes. A new part of her.

Let me be born, it whispers urgently, demanding.

Who are you?

Karma, proud and fierce the name.

What do you want?

Revenge, a voice that quivers inside in waves of satisfaction.

I want that too.

She dips the brush into the jar with paint and traces a line from the tip of her ear to her nose, over the bridge and up to the other ear. Another line, beneath it, thinner, stopping at her nostrils. Another underneath. A line from the middle of her bottom lip down on her chin. The paint covers some of her bruises.

A diamond shape in the middle of her forehead. She colours it in and removes a bit of paint with her finger, leaving two white horizontal spots. She smiles at her reflection.

This is going to be fun.

And bloody.

She picks up the pouch with the poison vials and the belt next to the discarded tunic and ties it to her waist again. Takes a torch from the wall and lights it from the lamp on the table. Underneath all the clothes in her chest, there's a smaller box filled with gold coins that she places in a cowhide, tying it to her waist as well. She surveys the room for a moment.

Then she sets fire to the tapestries on the walls, walks out and shuts the door behind her.

Her sisters and charges are where she left them, flowers withering on their chests. She touches the torch to each corner of the pyre and stands watch as the fire consumes the logs, the herbs, bursting and hissing as it sets the oils and creams aflame. She wants to imprint this moment in her memory.

The heat, the stench, the way their hair burns and their skin blisters in the heat. Their features, so familiar, so loved, melting into the skull, teeth, and empty sockets where their eyes shone. How fast their clothes turned to ashes, how their flesh smelled of meat, how charred their bones became, the soot, and the sparks that flow up into the night.

I see the Roman soldiers camped on the way to the forests of the East.

I want to trace their steps back to the West.

Who am I?

I am Karma, the soulless, remember? Rania is dead. She burned together with her sisters.

This is my story.

I am so hungry for blood and revenge.

I have nothing else to live for.

You know when you've done some exercise, danced, perhaps, and you sit down for a meal prepared for you, a meal that smells so good. Your mouth waters at the sight, with anticipation of the taste of each morsel, chewed quickly or slowly, filling your mouth with flavour.

So am I, standing here, watching the garrison in the distance.

Salivating.

They are mine to consume.

I will take my time.

I will enjoy every kill.

And

    I

        will

           have

              no

                mercy.

Titus

Birds sing the beginning of a new day. I get out of my tent and walk over to the edge of the camp, taking a leak. Look back towards the temple. See it burning. So she's still alive.

Interesting.

I couldn't sleep all night; that look of hers haunted my dreams. Coming and going. Screaming.

I tossed and turned. Finally gave up. It's time we get a move on and forget this whole situation. We got what we wanted.

I hear a horse's gallop approaching. It's a messenger from father asking for a report of our progress. He needs more income. The debtors from our lending houses, getting rich from sons going to war, are paying off their debts. Which means we cannot sell them and get more money. Return with riches he says or do not return at all. Very nice of him. Such fatherly concern.

I toss the letter into the fire and go get Cytheris. I need some cheering up.

She is asleep. I make my way into her bed and cuddle her, pulling my body close. She smells of last night's wine. So warm.

She mumbles something and caresses my arm. I hope to the gods she doesn't say the wrong name.

'Hey sweetheart.' She whispers, turning over, opening her eyes. Doesn't register any surprise at finding my face. She has been trained well. It pleases me.

'I am troubled, Cytheris. Make me forget. You're so good at making me forget.'

'What troubles you, Titus?'

'I have bad dreams.'

'What sort of dreams?'

'A priestess. One of the ones we defeated.'

'You cannot defeat a priestess, Titus. I hope you know that.'

'Of course I can. I did.'

'Is she dead?'

'No. She set fire to the temple.'

Cytheris smiles that knowing smile of hers. It annoys me.

'What are you smiling about?'

'The goddess works in mysterious ways, Titus. Perhaps you have met your match.'

'No woman is a match for me.'

'Perhaps you're right. You are a mighty man.'

'Don't mock me, whore.'

'Now, now. Please be at peace. Would you like some music?'

'Fine. Play something.'

She plays a song in a language I don't understand. Then translates, changing the tune slightly.

'When gods were forging the world.

And goddesses played with their hair.

Time itself stood still watching in rapture.

A gift for their beloveds, the world was.

An offering made with love.

The goddesses, pleased, started dancing.

The dance of life.'

'Nice.'

'Thank you.'

'Come, kiss me.'

She sets aside her cithara and lies next to me caressing my face.

'You are so beautiful.' She says.

It makes me smile.

I take her, ripping off her tunic, her body soft and yielding. I kiss and bite and suck at her skin. She opens up, moaning my name. I am inside and I am blind with the heat. The heat consumes my thoughts, my grunts remove all traces of last night's dream. On and on I push inside her, lost in her voice, her scent, her body. Such a good body. Mine, mine, mine.

She shushes soothingly. 'It's fine. You're safe. I am here. I am yours.'

Damn right she is.

Damn right.

Chapter 6 40 days and 40 nights

Karma

I am the desert wind that the dervishes fear. I am the woman howling at pain.

The first thing I need is information. So I walk west, tracing their steps back. The villagers are only too happy to share their troubles with who they think is Rania, there to heal their sorrows. I sit still while they talk, letting them give me all the knowledge that they've gathered. Listening to the silence between words. Seeing the images they try to describe. Knowing they will give me what I want.

'Rome, Rome, they kept on repeating this word,' One boy says. Children are so good at picking up knowledge. His mother chides him to be quiet.

'No, let him talk.' I command.

The boy blushes but is brave enough to speak.

'I'm sorry, priestess,' he says 'I did not understand everything they said. I do not speak their language.'

'It's fine,' I say, 'just tell me what you noticed.'

He noticed plenty. They are on a mission from a place called Rome to expand their territory and bring riches back to the city. We were not the first ones they treated so cruelly. Regulus is the name of their leader. Titus is the second in command. The boy also noticed that their army seems divided between the leaders.

'The men didn't get along very well,' he says quietly. 'They kept picking on each other, not like my friends and I do, but with a lot of anger in their voices.'

Anger. Anger is good. I can use that.

I say my goodbyes with proper ceremony.

'Are you going after them?' The boy asks as I leave.

I decide to tell him the truth.

'Yes.'

'I wish I could go with you.' He says puffing up his chest trying to appear manly and strong.

His mother pulls him back to her skirts. I bow to her in gratitude.

The next village confirms the boy's initial impressions. They are sorry that our temple burned. It is a bad omen. They do not know I set it on fire.

'Priestess, what are you going to do now?' A girl asks.

'I am going to learn their dialect.' I say.

'Oh, our teacher speaks their dialect.' She jumps up, excited to help. 'I'll call him.'

She runs off before I can stop her.

The teacher is a stooped old man, heavy and laden with age. There's sorrow in his lines. I have barely seen the features of the soldiers. Now, there's time to examine their type closer. Each tribe has a distinctive face and body. Although this man is old, his strength hasn't left him yet. His nose is large and proud. He shows me no respect. I decide to cut it short. I'll get the information somewhere else.

The next village at the foot of the mountains is the biggest I've been to. Their teacher is Greek. We exchange a few words in his language. He is more than happy to have someone to share his mother tongue with. I question him on his life and ask about this place called Rome.

'Ah Rome. I have been there once. Very beautiful city.'

'What of its people?'

'They like fighting. Fight each other all the time. Fight animals, fight slaves, fight neighbours.' His eyes twinkle with laughter. 'We the Greeks say they fight so much because their manhood is always questioned by their wives, who prefer Greek slaves to their husbands.' He slaps himself on the knee laughing. 'It's true. One of my cousins..'

I interrupt. 'Demetrios, what of their armies? Why are they sending their armies this way?'

'I don't know. The usual I suppose. Riches for the republic. Gold for the capital. Who knows the ambition of their king?' He eyes me. 'Why are you interested in their army?'

'The temple has some histories by Herodotus.' I say it by way of an answer. 'I am always curious if anything has changed since his time.' Smile on my face.

'Funny you say that.' He exclaims. 'I am a collector of histories myself. I have brought several scrolls from the scribes on my visit to Rome to read at leisure.' He leans in conspiratorially 'Would you like to see them?'

'Oh yes, please.' I say. 'That would make me very happy.'

He rushes out and comes back with a wooden chest. Blows the dust off and opens it. Takes out the first scroll and hands it to me with reverence.

'This one is my favourite.' He says. 'From their military school. It details their training philosophy. The codex of the soldier.'

'Demetrios, I did not expect you to have such refined tastes!' I say.

He puffs out his chest, proudly. 'I may be a simple teacher far from home, but my blood is still Greek.' He says.

'Thank you. May I have them for some time to study in detail?'

'Yes, yes. I would love to discuss it with you over wine when you've finished.'

'Oh, I certainly look forward to that.' I say standing up, taking my leave.

It takes me three days to copy the scrolls and tuck them in with my poisons. We discuss the Roman codex of the soldier. It places a lot of emphasis on honour. Dying for a greater cause.

Good. I can use that.

I need time alone. I need time to think. Talking to people is exhausting when all I want to do is scream. I am very close to losing it. It's best if I go into the wilderness for a while. It's best to let the screams out or they will interfere with my plan. Fortunately, the desert is very, very near.

Berenib, Nimra, and Saadia came from the desert. They described the passage through the mountains often on their visits to their home tribes. They said sand offered special healing power. I head in that direction, telling everyone that I was on a mission for the goddess and have no time to take advantage of their hospitality.

It's funny how long it takes people to see that you've changed. None of the families that housed me and called me Rania realised that the glint in my eye was not kind, nor was it from religious fervour. They fed me and gave me water and milk from their animals. They baked bread for me in the morning, an offering. They insisted I take provisions. I insisted they keep my coin in return as a bounty from the goddess. Coin makes people happy.

It's cold and uncomfortable in the mountains, especially when you sleep on the ground. My body was not used to rough stone, wind, and lack of running water. It ached and complained.

Many times a day I thought about returning. But I burned my bed and the image of my sisters' ashes was still imprinted on my mind's eye.

Mountains closing in on both sides, crows and goats curiously looking on, I keep going. Finally, the desert spreads before me, an ocean of sand and solitude. I walk straight into it, grab a handful of sand and let it run through my fingers. It is warm in the afternoon sun. I climb a dune and then another one. Dune after dune calls to me to immerse myself deeper into the arms of this vastness.

Alone. At last.

At night, the stars appeared dotting the sky with all the constellations that I knew. Sai used to point to one or another and name them. Sai is no more.

I fall asleep, weeping.

Sand and blinding sun, making my skin blister. Sweat, salty on my forehead. I walk and every step is agony. The bruises still hurt and I am still bleeding, raw from the rape.

Everything reminds me of what I had lost. Every breath I take was a breath in a world without my family.

Nights were the worst. Nights were when Ruth would come in for a cuddle, Leena sneak in for a chat, or Bianca for a laugh about her lovers. Nights were when my heart pulsed with the yearning to see them again. Nights were times when I had no answer to why I was alive. Why was love not enough? I am getting to know these new men.

Morning, a hawk is circling above me. I follow it deeper into the sands. It becomes unbearably hot. I am thirsty. I climb another dune and face the sand in all directions, screaming.

Adonae, adonae. Why have you abandoned me?

Silence.

The goddess has nothing to say at this time.

I found an oasis. Water, gushing from the ground, murmuring soft lullabies. Birds chirp washing themselves in the pond framed by date palms, branches heavy with harvest. I grab a handful, chewing fast, swallowing the sweetness, gulping down the water till my belly protests with a burp.

I gather some more water in the cup of my hands and splash it on my face, letting it run down to my neck, to my chest, cooling, soothing my pain. It feels good. My tunic feels heavy, dirty, uncomfortable. I let it fall off my shoulders, feeling the sun warm my skin.

I look down at my breasts. The right one has bruises, from fingers grabbing roughly. I examine it closer, noticing the scratches left by dirty nails, the memory of caked blood, my blood, covering the wounds while they heal. I pour water on it, gently caressing it with my hand, cupping it and holding it, feeling its softness. My breasts. I reclaim my body as my own. Every inch of it. I know how. Examining further with curiosity, I observe my body.

The left one, slightly bigger, has a knife slit wound below the nipple. I hold it too, feeling my finger against torn tissue, the warmth of my palm spreading deep, enveloping the ache I'd stopped paying attention to. I pour water on it. It stings, letting me know I'm alive. I chew a stem from a palm leaf, mixing the bitter taste with my saliva and paste it over the gash. Place my right arm on it, count my heartbeat. One, two, three, four, five. My breasts.

Gather more water and hold my face, touching the temples, noticing each stab of pain from a bruise. Forehead, round, welcoming the coolness of water, cheekbones, sore, left eye, swollen, tears, falling, everything aches. I let the sobs come, searching for an end to despair, finding none. One breath, deep breath, brings me back. Blowing my nose hurts because it's broken.

'Fuuuuck youuuuuuuuu!' I scream into the sky. 'Fuuuuuuuuck.' The sound, letting out all the sadness, becomes anger. Another scream. Longer this time. Anger becomes rage, digging deep into my core, lower, growling now. From my womb the next roar comes, like the lions that I heard three nights ago, my whole body tensing, and then releasing everything that is not pure, sharp fury.

It fills me with strength that I breathe in. I let out another roar. Here, roaring in the middle of an oasis in the desert, I give myself up to the primordial sounds that come, come, consuming everything.

I roar at the palm trees, at the pond, at the dunes, at the sun, at the sky, in all directions. I roar at the memories that come, not chasing them away. At the faces of my sisters, at the smiles of the girls, at the soldiers, coming in, screaming, with that look in their eyes.

I roar at the punches, at feeling powerless, at how I couldn't stop them. At how my whole body struggled to escape, at how I cried out for the goddess, at how I cried out stop, stop, stop, no, no, no, stop, stop, no, stop, please, stop.

I roar at how they did not stop, at how none of the eyes I looked into, pleading, had any compassion, or understanding of my pain.

I roar with a fury that is boundless and keeps coming and coming till all images disappear and all sounds disappear, till the world disappears and I find myself in a black, boundless darkness.

It is excruciating to have parts of you that were open, loving, and one with everything, shatter.

The problem with that is not that you die – death is of course an illusion. The problem is - you lose the part of you that's connected to everything. You lose instant access to universal knowing, access to the rhythms of life around you. You fall from unity and oneness. You become separate; alone; scared. And instead of joy, life becomes about survival.

Of the fittest, fastest, smartest, quickest. Whatever works.

The roars don't stop the next day. Nor the next. I drink. I feed myself on plants and animals. I scream into the night. Night after night. I try to gouge my eyes out, I try to peel my skin off with my fingernails. I pull at my hair. I convulse on the ground, shaking. Anything to make the pain stop. It doesn't. So I scream. It is the only relief.

One morning, as I lie back on the sand, arms spread wide looking through the palm fronds at the sky, watching the breeze and the fronds caress each other, the screams stop, giving place to grief. Heavy like a marble column, it pins me to the ground so I can't move.

Suddenly, I hear laughter. Hyenas.

I watch them circle me, ready to attack. I crouch swiftly, knife in hand, ready. One lunges at me from behind. I stick my blade in her throat before she can land. Take her by her hind leg and use her body to beat the others away, teeth bared, growling. I rip her fur off, suck in her blood, and bite into the raw warm flesh.

The fuckers skimp away whining.

'Retreat, retreat.' I cackle after them.

Who am I? I am Karma, the soulless.

I am done screaming.

'We all agreed to this. In the gathering of souls it was decided that we will play a darker game.

We played it to perfection. Every single step of the way.'

Letters

Leader

Regulus sighs. The letter he received from his brother-in-law revealed the latest changes in the senate. *Titus' family is becoming more powerful*, it said. *They have aligned themselves with the king's brother through marriage. Should the king die before you return, they will be first in line to rule. Make sure you take charge of this mission and return with wealth and territory. We have much to lose if you don't. Your wife sends her regards. She too is anxious for the success of your expedition. She says her brother the king is receiving new treatment for his affliction but is not certain if the improvement will last. Your son is now enrolled at school, getting training in combat, as was decreed by you before you left. I urge you to return victorious. Your future as king depends on it.*

He lets the parchment fall into his lap. 'Onix,' He calls out to a mountain of a man standing at the entrance. 'Please tell Titus I want to see him and his men in my tent.'

Onix bows before leaving to obey his orders.

Good man, Onix. He thinks to himself. Even after we overtook his party on the way to the temple and sent the little girl he was travelling with to Lucrezia, he promised me loyalty. Serving the goddess, as he explained. I need the goddess on my side now. More than ever.

Titus and six of his men come into the tent, sombre.

'You called?' Titus speaks first.

'I hear congratulations are in order. Your sister's marriage is an excellent match.'

'And here I thought you were a fool who knows nothing. Yes, she married well.'

'Congratulations.'

'Is that why you called me here?' He asks impatiently.

'No.'

'What is it then?'

'I have heard reports that your men have taken more than their share of the loot from the temple.'

'Have you now? And who was stupid enough to tell you such a lie?'

'I trust my men. They wouldn't lie to me.'

'A fool and his trust are easy to manipulate.'

'Titus, I've had enough of your insults. We are in this together. We both have much to lose if we are not successful. Fights between our men will weaken us. The enemy could take advantage.'

'What enemy? The villagers we've encountered?'

Regulus sighs, closing his eyes for a moment. How can he make him see?

'Titus. Who taught you the art of war?' He asks finally.

'No one. It's in my blood. Mars fucked my great great grandmother.'

Regulus is speechless. He tries again.

'Titus. Men. So far we have encountered no enemy to match our strength. But these were farmers, not soldiers. Sooner or later we will have to face a city and a king. Sooner or later we will have to face our match. If we are not united, we will be defeated.'

'Says who?'

'This is the first strategy of war, Titus. Divide and conquer. We use it. We will be fools to have it used against us.'

'I am no fool.'

'Then control your men.' He says testily. 'Or you will make fools of both of us.'

'Is that all?'

'Yes.'

Chapter 7 Desert Rose

Karma

I had been walking for seven days without encountering any human alive. The skins and woven tunics that tribe women provided kept me warm and cool. My water was running out.

I find bodies that lay half buried in the sand. I ransack them for gold and coin and leave the rest to the buzzards. Most of them died bleeding, of wounds that could have easily been cured.

The old man looks dead but when I turn him, he lets out a hiss of breath. I look him over. No wounds, dehydrated. Not a soldier. He opens his eyes, squinting from the glare. Movements slow, I take out my meagre reserves of water and let a few drops on his cracked lips. He licks them with a dried out tongue, mouth opening for more. I pour more water, never taking my eyes off his. They are black like the night. He sits up and coughs. I wait till it subsides. Give him another gulp. Observe him fill his mouth till his cheeks puff. He takes small, small sips observing me.

'Shukriya.' His voice croaks gratitude. His eyes do not warm with emotion.

'Jhayasha?' I ask, making sure my face only reveals the question. 'Was it the legion that caused you to be in this state?'

He registers no surprise at my knowing. Women helping him out in the desert and asking about armies must be a regular thing in his life.

'No, I was left behind by my caravan, my partners left like thieves in the middle of the night. Sons of hyenas, may the slaves fuck their mothers.' He spits out the curse in the direction his caravan must have taken. 'I was returning home when my strength left me. I was making peace with the creator and then you appeared.'

He scans me, registering the skins and the tunic and my braided hair as I tie the water pouch back to my belt.

'You're not a tribe woman.' He states.

'La – no.' I do not volunteer more information.

'May the gods reward you for saving my life.'

I nod, accepting.

'You don't talk much, do you?' His eyes narrow, deciding whether to trust me or not. He decides to trust his instinct. His face breaks out into the warmest smile.

'God is great and I am a great sinner for not accepting his mercy.'

Then, placing a hand on his heart, he continues.

'Please, do me the honour of accompanying me to my family. It would give them great pleasure to thank you for saving my life.'

'Where is it?'

'A day or two from here. If it weren't for you, I would have died so close to home, it would be too much of a joke. We will throw a great feast. Please, allow me this honour to have you stay with us and rest for a few days. Replenish your supplies before you continue on your journey.'

My gut tells me this is a good idea.

'The honour would be mine to come and meet your family. I am grateful for the hospitality.' I accept. 'The gods favour me too by our meeting.'

I stand up. I offer my hand to help him up. He refuses it.

'Your water gives me great strength, thank you.' He lifts himself up and points north. 'This way please.'

We walk, sand running rivulets around our feet. The sun is beginning to set to our left, casting shadows onto the dunes. Yellow becomes orange, the air becomes cooler, transparent, as if absent. The heat is being removed from around us, sucked out slowly.

'What is your name? I'm sorry, I haven't asked before.' He says, uncomfortable with the silence.

'Karma.' I replied. The name makes him shiver.

'Powerful name. I heard from traders that it means revenge in some religions, far to the east.'

'It can mean that, yes.'

'Was it given to you by your parents or did you choose it?'

I do not want to answer his question, so I stay silent. From the corner of my eye, I see him looking up at me, opening his mouth to insist. No sound escapes his lips. He looks to the ground, sighs deeply and says.

'My parents named me Kareem. It means generous.'

That makes me smile. A man who knows when not to insist. I like this one.

'You are generous.' I say smiling at him.

He nods his thanks. The smile we share is genuine. We relax and walk in silence, watching the sky morph till the sun reaches the horizon.

'Let us set camp. This is your homeland. Where would you suggest we make our fire?'

'Down there near the valley, at the bottom of this dune. It will protect us from the wind and we can find dried weeds to feed it.'

'Lead the way.'

I drop my sack on the ground to mark the spot where we are to take shelter for the night. Kareem doubles, supporting himself on his knees, fighting hunger and nausea. Breathing into his belly. Slowly, he stands upright. I hand him the water skin. He fills his mouth letting the skin inside absorb the water before gulping it down. He hands it back to me, insisting on returning it when I offer he take another sip.

'There won't be enough for the two of us if I take another sip. This is enough to sustain us till we reach my family. Then we can drink till our bellies ache.'

'Good.' I say.

'Do you like stories?' he asks after a pause.

'They pass the time.'

'I ask because I know of a story that reminds me of our situation.'

'What is it about?'

'A guy in the desert.' He replies smiling. 'Talking to a burning bush.'

'He must have been crazy.'

'Yeah. Like us.'

We laugh.

As soon as the fire is crackling happily, we settle to share the bread and cheese that I bring out of my sack. Munching slowly, we exchange smiles and break into spontaneous laughter. At the silence, at our newly formed bond, at the absurdity of how we met. At the way our paths crossed, bringing together such different lives. Burning bushes in the desert. Crazy.

Revenge and generosity. Sharing a meal. Not k-i-s-s-i-n-g .

We cannot stop, we are rolling on the ground, with tears streaming down our cheeks.

I guess you had to be there.

Waradya liked me from the first moment she set her eyes on me. I could tell by her shy smile that she hid behind the veil. Kareem had hugged her close and pushed her towards me with:

'This is my daughter, my rose, Waradya.'

'Daughter, this is Karma, she saved my life. Truly, your father would be eaten by jackals if it weren't for her.'

'Welcome to our home.' She says.

'Come, come, let's prepare a place for Karma and a feast, we must have a feast!' Kareem exclaims as he walks into the middle of the camp holding on to Waradya's shoulder.

Huts built with canvas and wood are grouped in a circle around a central fire pit. Men, women, and children are leaving their chores and coming out to greet Kareem.

'Hello, hello,' he laughs at the hugs. 'This is Karma, she saved my life.'

'Welcome Karma,' each person says in different tones, eyeing me curiously.

'Blue eyes,' they whisper and smile. There aren't many of them. This clan is composed of Kareem, his two elder brothers with their families; their cousins from their mother's side, their cousin's from their father's side, two sets of grandmothers, one grandfather and children, too numerous to count. They run around naked, screaming and laughing.

They bring water and bread for us to eat. Kareem leaves off shouting directions. Waradya takes me into a tent to wash up and change.

'Thank you for saving my father's life. I am forever in your debt.' She looks calm saying it. She looks like she knows the meaning of forever.

'My pleasure.'

She leaves me with a basin filled with warm water, oil, perfume, and a fresh tunic to change into.

'Waradya, have you heard of a place called Rome?' I ask her when she comes back.

'No.' She says. 'But I don't travel with the caravans. Father might know.'

He doesn't.

I wonder why I'm here.

Waradya

It's night. I lay on a dune just outside our oasis watching the stars. I think about my fiancée, Amir. We've known each other since he gave me chicken bones to suck when I was teething, our mothers too busy tending to the rest of the family to deal with my cries. He was sitting outside his tent, finishing a drumstick when he saw me naked, on the ground, snot filling my mouth. He waddled towards me and handed me the bone. I took it but kept crying a little more, at least that's the way he told that story.

'I was only four but I remember you wouldn't shut up.' He'd tease. 'Just like now.'

'You can't tease me about that forever, you know.'

'You just watch. When you're my wife, I can tease you about anything I want.'

I pretend I want to hit him and chase after him for a while.

His laughter died for some reason when he saw my father and that woman, Karma, entering the camp. I thought it was because he was afraid of the news my father would bring. Afraid his cousins who left with the caravan had died. But he wouldn't take his eyes off her. Which meant I wanted to examine her a little closer too.

Blue eyes, she looked at me with her blue eyes when father introduced us. She looked at me as if she could see into the depth of my soul. She looked at me and I was struck, standing motionless, barely able to respond.

I was forever in her debt for saving father of course, but if I were honest with myself I just wanted to be around her. Forever. Wherever. I didn't care. She made me feel. She made my body shiver and go from hot to cold without control. When she brushed her arm against mine, goosebumps filled my skin, my hair standing on end. I was on fire. I was consumed by her presence, her voice, her laughter. I was lost in her eyes. There was no explanation for it. If she was a sorceress and this was a spell then I was happy to be so spellbound. All of a sudden, my world was enlightened, senses heightened, every colour brighter, every birdsong sweeter. She existed. She was here. Nothing else mattered.

Amir noticed. My father noticed. Everyone noticed. You had to be blind not to see the sparkle in my eyes. I followed her around everywhere. She stayed in my tent. I watched her sleep and wake up, morning light on her skin, lips slightly parted. Her smell. It was intoxicating. It was more fragrant than flowers. It enveloped me. I wanted to drown in it.

I brushed her hair and helped her dress. I brought her water to wash and the perfumes I was saving for my wedding night. My best tunics, my best scarves, the undergarments meant for my life as wife – I gave it all to her without a second thought. Nothing made me as happy as watching her wear it. A part of me on her.

There were bruises on her skin and scars that were only beginning to heal. Once, when I was rubbing oils into her body, after a bath, I asked about the scars.

'I don't want to talk about it.' She said in a dry tone.

I didn't ask again. My hands on her body. Warm palms, oiled with coconut and rose oils, the scent of myrrh burning in the tent. I slide over her back, easing the pressure around the bruises and the wounds. I feel my way, eyes closed, from the tip of her fingers, to the hardness of her elbow, down to the muscles of her forearms. My fingertips perceive the rough hair under her armpits. She giggles as I slide them down to her ribs. The sound sends a heatwave into my body. She stands and turns around to face me. Naked. I can't take my eyes off of her. Her breasts have more cuts on them. Tentatively, I slide my finger lightly over the wounds. Open my mouth to ask. Change my mind.

She takes my hand in hers. Draws me close. Caresses my cheek, tracing a line along my jaw to my chin. Lifts my face. I have to look into her eyes. I forget myself because suddenly, her lips are on mine.

And I.

I.

I explode.

Birth

It was Waradya who realised I was pregnant. She was holding my breast in the morning, waiting for me to wake up, her nose buried in the nape of my neck, inhaling the scent of my hair.

'Karma, I think you're with child.' She whispers.

I knew. Of course I knew. My womb was heavy, engrossed in its sacred task. It was familiar to me, that fullness. Waves of peace and pure creation emanating from it. Waves of power. I didn't want to admit it, even to myself. Now, there it was, the knowing undeniable.

A child of force. The universe did not make love to itself in its conception. The universe was vile and brutal and destructive. There was nothing but pain in the memory of two becoming one. Nothing but complete denial of all that is pure and beautiful in this world.

I sat up, placing my hands on my womb. Felt into the life growing there. I knew exactly what to do.

'Waradya, I will need some herbs for this. Does your midwife use any that grow nearby?'

'I'll ask.' She replies.

A few hours later she returns with an old stooped woman, with a half shut eye. She looks at me sideways, her black eyes taking me all in.

'You're with child all right.' She says.

'Yes, I know.'

'Not your first?'

'If you help me, there won't be any.'

With raised eyebrows she continues. 'Waradya here tells me you're looking for some herbs. Are they to heal you or the child?'

'The herbs are to heal me and get rid of the child.'

She purses her lips. Knowing enough not to ask or insist. Sighs.

'It is not what I enjoy most,' she says. 'I enjoy helping bring life.' She pauses, observing me carefully. Tentatively, she continues 'But life is meant to be brought in joy and compassion...' She trails off.

'This would be a life borne of pain.' I say.

She steps back, startled. Approaches me surprisingly quickly for a woman of her age and hugs me close.

'You will not have to bear a life of pain.' She whispers. 'Not if I have anything to do with it.'

Stepping back and looking up at me. 'Don't you worry. Everything is going to be alright.'

I relax. The goddess is on my side. She sent her crone to soothe me.

'Come to me tomorrow at dawn and we will start. Tell everyone you're on a journey with me, not to be disturbed for three days.' Then, she commands 'Waradya, make sure no one comes into my tent.'

She pats my hands.

'See you tomorrow, dearie. Don't you worry, old Khtur will take good care of you.'

Waradya wakes me up with a trail of kisses on my neck. I stretch, luxuriating in the sensation. She nestles herself in my arms, hugging me close. Caressing my belly, she whispers.

'Goodbye baby, I hope you come back at a better time soon.'

I tighten my grip around her. 'Thank you.'

'Of course. I love you. I won't let anything bad happen to you.'

'Thank you.'

Khtur's tent is some distance away from all the others. Draped in red silk fabric on the inside, all her possessions set around a fire hearth in the middle, cauldron boiling, smoke coming out through the hole in the roof.

Rows of dried herbs are strung across the ceiling. I notice a chest filled with her tools. I know enough of healing to recognize a fellow master of the craft. She's holding a bunch of sage, the smoke clearing the air, preparing for the ritual. I feel safe. I'm in good hands.

'Come, come, sit.' She indicates some pillows on the floor. 'How are you feeling?'

'Good. A little scared. I've never done this before.'

She smiles. 'You have a beautiful, strong body,' she says. 'I will show you what I will use and explain what to expect. Yes?'

'Yes.'

She gathers a pillow off the floor and places it on top of another in front of me. Plops herself down, leans in, takes my hand into both of hers and looking me straight in the eyes says:

'You're not doing anything wrong. It is against life and nature to bring a child of pain into the world. You are a being of joy and light. You have the right to be free. Yes.'

I nod.

She continues.

'We want to make this as painless as possible for you. So right now, your womb is lined with a layer, filled with blood and other lines feeding the new life inside. If there were no life inside you this lining would peel away naturally and come out. You know this, yes?'

I nod.

'And so what we must do now is ask the womb to release the lining, together with the little ball of flesh that it is feeding at the moment. Just as if there was nothing there. Yes?'

'Yes.'

'Are your menses usually painful?'

'No.'

'Good, good. That is very good news! That means you're at peace with yourself. Right. This makes my job easier.'

She settles in more comfortably into the pillows and brings my hand closer.

'Here's what we're going to do. I will place three different drinks in front of you. Each one has a mix of special herbs to help you with letting the lining and the flesh go. There is an order to drink them but your womb knows better what it needs than I, yes?'

I nod, quickly, listening.

'Here's what you need to do. You place your left hand on your womb and ask it to assist you with this. Acknowledge its power and its right to creation. Send it love and compassion. Tell it you are not ready. Tell it it needs to let go of this creation. Then, after you get her agreement, drink from the cup that feels best to you. After that, lie down for a nap.'

'That's it?'

'That's it.'

I do what she says. I thank my womb for her power of creation. I thank her for giving me so many children of joy. I tell her I am not ready now. I feel its sadness. I feel its compassion. I feel it letting go. I remember to connect with the new life growing inside me.

'There is nothing but pain in the creation of your flesh', I whisper. 'You can come back when there is only love in the creation of your flesh.' I wait.

The flesh doesn't mind the pain. 'Come back when there is only love in the creation of your flesh,' I repeat. I wait.

'Life is precious,' it whispers.

'Come back when there is only love in the creation of your precious life.' I say again.

'I don't know what that is,' the child answers.

'Choose anybody who is engaged in pure love in the creation of flesh and find out.' I gave it the option.

'I want you,' the child insists.

'I can't and won't give birth to you right now.' I say. 'You cannot make this decision for me.'

Respectfully, the soul relents. I reclaim the last of my body from the violence.

Slowly, I take the cup in the middle and drink the warm liquid. I feel relief and support. I feel my womb relaxing and opening, preparing for menses. I lie back into the pillows, place my other hand on my lower belly, close my eyes, and tune in deeper into my body.

Khtur starts humming a tune. She goes to her chest and takes out a small drum, pacing around me, patting the stretched skin. I smell rain. I fall asleep. I dream I am floating in the air, looking down at my body spread out on the pillows, at Khtur circling around me. I feel light and soft. Peaceful. I don't need to go anywhere, just be here in this hut.

The singing and the drumming gets louder and I wake up with the sensation of having fallen to the ground after flying. I am feverish.

'Drink the second cup,' says Khtur without pausing her dance or the drumming. I roll to one side and take a sip from the cup closest to me. It tastes bitter, brings up bile, and I throw up.

'Keep drinking.' Khtur insists.

I know enough about purging fever to agree with her order. Releasing the contents of my stomach makes me feel better. The second time I drink the liquid, the bitterness has a layer of sweetness on top. It feels good. I finish the cup and lay back to rest.

I am in a dream almost immediately. At peace. I feel no pain. Hours pass, Khtur drumming, singing, and humming. Khtur, dear Khtur, her voice deep and soft and kind. Dear Khtur, leading me on this journey.

The second time I wake up there is no fever. My body feels numb. I look down between my legs. There's blood and a ball of flesh. I wrap it in fresh linen that she laid next to me and set it aside.

'Drink the last cup.' She says.

I am strong enough to sit up. I drink the cup. It tastes of mint and cherries. I lay back and fall into a deep sleep. This time I see nothing. Khtur keeps drumming.

Two more days and two more nights I spend with Khtur in her tent. She feeds me. She shares her wisdom. We go on another journey together. I see a knife, the blade sharp, the hilt surrounded by entwined snakes, golden serpents with red glowing eyes. I see a golden goblet, encrusted with rubies. I see myself wearing a silk tunic, light and see-through.

On the fourth morning it's Waradya who wakes me up. Khtur is nowhere to be seen. I look around, confused.

'She said you were ready.' Says Waradya by way of explanation.

I look at the breakfast tray that she set beside me. Steaming tea flavoured with cardamom, flat bread, butter, cheese and a ripe, plump peach. I sit up, cross legged and spread the cheese on the bread.

'How's the preparation for your wedding going?' I ask her, taking a bite.

She looks down, blushing.

'Good. Father is very happy. Everyone is very happy.'

'And you?'

There's so much love in her eyes as she looks at me.

'I am where I want to be,' she says. 'With you.'

'Waradya, no.'

Her body slumps at the words.

'I am done here. I must go on. You can't come with me.'

'I can. I can help you. I can be by your side. I can.'

'No,' I interrupt, 'I'm doing this alone. You do what you need to do. I don't want you where I'm going. Stay here, where you're safe.'

Her eyes fill with tears.

'But. I love you.'

'I know. It's not enough. There's no room in my journey for you. None. Understand?'

She nods, unconvinced. She thinks she can lie to me. I look at her, long and hard. No words will convince her. So be it. I will show her.

'Waradya, I need a horse. I'll come back soon. In time for your wedding. Go. Bring me a horse.'

She obeys. I finish my breakfast. Look around for the linen bundle. Find it behind me.

Go out into the desert and bury it under a thorn bush.

Sit in silence, trying to feel something.

There's nothing. I clap my hands once, ending this chapter.

'When you start chasing darkness, you become like it. There is no other way.'

Letters

Chapter 8 Killing me softly

Titus

Who does he think he is, telling me what to do with my own men? I am the great descendant of Mars, the god of war. His blood runs in my veins. I will not stand for this.

'Cato.' I bark at my sergeant. 'Follow me.'

'Yes, sire.' He says as he walks into my tent behind me.

I turn around to face him.

'My informant tells me there's a village not far from here. It's trading season. Plenty of caravans gathered to sell their wares – a good opportunity for more bounty for our men. While our leader decides which way to go, we can take this opportunity to have some fun.'

'Who shall we take with us?' asks Cato.

'Our men and our men only.'

'What about Regulus?'

'I'll inform him. Have the men ready to leave after the meal.'

'Yes.' Cato stands erect, nods, executes a military turn and walks off to obey.

Just the way I like it.

The market is busy with people tasting food, buying cattle, haggling with the butcher, and cries of invitations to sample exotic spices from faraway lands.

Children are running around chasing each other. Women finger trinkets at the jeweller's stall, trying silk and wool fabrics against their chests while their men look on grimly at the sellers trying to calculate how much it's going to cost them.

We walk in formation, stepping in unison, slowly approaching the middle of the square. People are shying away, looking on. The plaza falls silent. A baby's cries pierce the air. An old beggar with a cane approaches us to ask for alms.

I look at Cato, to my right. Nod. He is quick. His short sword pierces the old man's heart, ending his miserable life. Everyone starts screaming and running away.

'Attack!' I yell as I charge the body nearest to me.

The rush. The smell of blood. The feel of sword piercing flesh. The cries for mercy. A growl escapes me. I want more. I will not be satisfied till every soul in this village is with the gods. I hear Mars laughing uproariously. I am Mars; I laugh too.

'Have mercy for my baby, please, please.' A woman is pleading at one of my men as he picks it up by its leg, high in the air and cuts into him.

'No.' She screams, throwing herself on his leg, mad with grief, she bites into it, tearing off flesh.

The soldier screams, plunging the sword into her back.

I approach.

'You let yourself be wounded by a woman.' I say. 'You are a shame to the empire.'

With that, I cut off both his legs. My sword is sharp. It loves blood.

The plunging and pillaging continues. We set fire to the stalls, the houses, the animals; till everything is soot and fire, smoke and screams.

Finally, when there's nothing but the sound of the roaring flames, we stop. We gather at the edges of the village, watching our handiwork.

I smile at my men.

'We've done well.'

'But, sir, there is no bounty left.' Pipes up one of my soldiers.

'Didn't you have fun?' I ask, looking at him.

He backs away, bowing in silence. Far from my reach.

'Back to camp, the lot of you.'

'We think the gods are nice. We think that only kindness and love exists in their realms. And human suffering belongs to mortal sins. You will not be judged for your actions in some mysterious afterlife where you will burn in hell for eternity. This is the life where you reap what you sow. For every choice you make.'

Letters

Karma

To kill or not to kill is never the question. The true question is how.

Before we go into details, dear soul, you need to let go of everything you think you know about murder.

Taking a life is not so hard for the soulless.

We're about to go down the rabbit hole.

All you can do is watch, observe and enjoy the ride.

Butterflies.

Dragonflies.

Sweet kisses.

Rage. Rage burns and consumes, giving power.

The Roman centurion left a lot of fear in their wake. Clouds of dark smoke, not just from hundreds of broken villages that they laid to waste but from the killed and the wounded. Fear hung in the air like a thick blanket falling on everything and everyone. It paralysed resistance. It twisted the minds of people into imagining the worst possible outcomes. It turned them into losers even before the battle took place.

Some gods feed on fear. To them, fear is sweeter than opium. It's like an orgasm in your whole body. Seeing someone give you their power. Provoke it. Control them through it.

Here's how. First, you place the idea of fear in someone's mind, perhaps by appearing slightly bigger than you are. A simple thought of fear is enough.

Something primal in them will stir, when they see the madness in your eyes. Some cellular memory of being persecuted, maimed, or killed. Then the emotion of fear will overtake their bodies. You can absorb it immediately or take your time. I used to take my time, sipping it slowly, stroke their ego while I'm at it and they'd give me more.

I was not afraid. Never afraid. Those on the other side of fear only know power. Those on the other side of fear love that you think power is evil. What will they do, after all, when you realise your fear is your own to sample and use? How will they survive if every single one of you takes your power back? My rage fed on that fear. It's the strongest kindling for its fire. I learned to love it. I learned to hunt it out in my victims, smell it out, provoke it, feed on it, sucking it in with lust.

Each kill brought its lesson.

It's of vital importance that you acknowledge what it's like to have power over others. The sweetness of it. It is imperative you acknowledge your attraction to giving your power away with absolute abandon. The freedom of it. Both are constant parameters within which we all play the victim, tyrant and saviour roles.

Yes, it's all a game.

And I love winning.

It is still summer. The air is dry against my skin, hot wind blowing constantly against my cheeks. A village, burned down to the ground, wisps of smoke from charred huts, a fire still feeding on one pillar or another. Bodies slowly decompose in the heat. An abandoned dog barks then runs away, tail between its legs.

I hear a sound. A human sound. A soldier, left to die wounded. His legs are cut off and he is dragging himself on the ground to the nearest well. The black scars of the burned down village set off the red trail he leaves behind. I approach as he stops to face me. I remember him. His fist on my face. His hands on my thighs.

First one, races through my mind. It has begun.

I pick up a rock and advance. He brings out a blade. It's a work of art, with an ornate holder of two snakes entwined. A ritual blade. Familiar blade. He thinks he can defend himself against me.

I let the rock drop. Pick up a spear from the ground that lies discarded. Must have been his. Step by step I inch closer to him, my hand getting used to the feel of wood, round and deadly. I become one with it. I see him screaming and giving me his fear. In my mind, I already killed him. All I have to do now is watch. All I have to do now is enjoy how it happens.

He looks at me. A flicker of understanding flashes through his eyes. He remembers me. I can sense his agreement to be killed. At a soul level, this is his end. Knowing illuminates my entire being. I know how. A sort of curiosity overtakes me. The sense of reality changes. My new path clear. Do I want to take it? My pain requires an outlet. I take it. I can see his death at my hand. At that moment, I made a choice. He attempts to defend himself. His pride as a Roman soldier gives him strength. At least he will die with honour, in battle, I can hear what he thinks. Unfortunately, there is no honour in death. Not even of a soldier. So I caused him only pain. Only humiliation. I follow my knowing to the letter.

Swiftly, I stick the spear in his left thigh and without pause pull it out and pierce his right thigh, push against it with all my weight, pinning him to the ground. He screams, raising his face to the heavens, the scream flying out into the sky. He drops the dagger.

Blood, he looks at his own blood and back to me, wide eyed. In horror. 'What are you?' He asks. 'Death,' I say. 'I came for you.'

He struggles to understand.

I don't want to end it just yet. I take him by his hair and drag him to the charred post of a hut, binding him to it. There's plenty of kindling strewn about. I gather it, slowly, placing it under what is left of his legs. He tries to remove it but it hurts too much. He begs me, 'No. Please kill me, kill me now. Isn't it what you want? Kill me with that dagger. I beg you. Please. No, no, stop it. Please. Please. Please.'

I tune his voice out, concentrating on my task. One of the huts is still burning. I light a stick – an old man's cane and bring it to the pyre.

The fire catches quickly – it hasn't rained in a long time.

He screams. His flesh smells of cooked meat, it sizzles, bubbles. I watch closely as he convulses, trying to get away, hurting himself more, always screaming in pain and rage. I remember how hungry I am. I walk away.

Pick up the dagger. It is warm in my hands, my fingers comfortable around the hilt.

I come back to watch him burn. Add more wood to the fire.

He dies too quickly for my taste.

I make a note to not wound the next one.

It's over. I am filled. For now.

It's a brave new world and I know I'll be hungry for more.

'All is well.

All is always well.'

Letters

Tribe

The air is abuzz with talk of the upcoming wedding between Waradya and Amir. Women are sitting outside their tents, sewing dresses for the celebration. Men are preparing to go hunting for meat.

'How long does the feast last?' Karma asks Waradya.

'Usually a week.' she replies 'I don't want to get married.' She looks down at her hands.

'And what do you want to do?' Karma takes her hands and forces her to look up. 'Tell me, what is it that you want to do, Waradya?'

'I want to come with you. I want to follow you, wherever you go. I can cook for you, I can mend your clothes.' She pauses. 'I can love you.'

'If you know what's good for you - ' Karma trails off. 'Oh what's the point?' She looks away, making a decision. 'I'll tell you what, tomorrow you can come with me.'

Waradya lights up. 'Really?'

'Yes.'

Kareem approaches them.

'Oh Karma, I hope you'll stay for the wedding. I am a happy, happy man. My dear Rose is getting married and will bring me many grandchildren!' He laughs. 'I can already see them running around calling me grandpa.' He looks at his daughter. 'Why, I can see you're happy too. Look at those eyes shining. No wonder. Amir is a good man.'

Waradya blushes deeply. 'Papa, Karma is taking me tomorrow on one of her trips.'

Kareem's face falls as he faces both of them, looking from one to the other.

'What is the meaning of this? Where are you taking my daughter?'

'She wants to come with me.' Karma replies 'I see no reason to refuse her. She is curious about my doings.'

'Curiosity is not a good thing, Waradya. You should be ashamed of yourself, running off into the desert, such a short time before your wedding. What will your cousins say about me? I'll tell you what they'll say. They'll say I cannot control my own daughter and that I am a useless old man.' He is getting angry.

Khtur comes out of the tent to their left and hurries over to Kareem's side.

'What is it, Kareem? What has gotten you so upset today? You should be celebrating!' She asks with a twinkle in her eye.

'These two are running off into the desert tomorrow, on my horses no doubt.' He points at the two women. His eyebrows shoot up with indignation. 'Have you ever heard of such a thing? Such a short time before the wedding!'

Khtur narrows her eyes shrewdly. She looks at Karma, who is sitting relaxed, unperturbed by the man's anger. Waradya, blushing a deep red is hunched up, making herself as small as possible.

'Don't you trust the woman who saved your life?' She asks finally.

This calms him down. Still, he is unsure. He mumbles. 'These things, Khtur, are very strange. Karma saved my life, yes. She is free to do as she wishes. But Waradya. Waradya has never been alone outside of this place. What if something happens to her? What will we do then?' He turns to Khtur.

'It's dangerous out there. There are wars, marauding tribes, and wild animals. Who will protect her? No, no.' He turns to Karma. 'You know I am grateful to you for saving my life, but I cannot let you take my daughter with you. She is my responsibility.'

Karma smiles.

'So she is.' And says no more.

Waradya starts to plead, 'But father, I...'

'No, Waradya. I have made up my mind. You are not going anywhere.'

Khtur takes Karma by the hand.

'Come with me.' She says. 'We must speak.'

They walk into her tent, she makes sure no one follows them and closes the flap.

Turning to look at Karma she says.

'You've killed a man.'

It's not a question.

'Yes.' Replies Karma calmly.

'You enjoyed it.'

'Yes.'

'Is this your way now, priestess?'

'Yes.'

'So be it.'

She walks to her wooden chest.

'Do you need anything?'

'Yes. Poison.'

'How much?'

'Enough to kill a hundred men.'

Karma

The wounded they left served as experiments.

'Will you ever stop?' Waradya awaits my return with food and tea. She asks this every time I come back.

'Stop what?'

'Going away.'

I look at her. She's assuming I'm staying. The fool.

'I will leave before your wedding and never come back.'

She stays quiet for a few moments, looking at her hands, neatly folded in her lap. Tears are streaming down her face, falling one by one, being absorbed by the fabric of her dress.

'I don't know why I love you.' She says quietly. I can barely hear her.

'I didn't ask you to love me. That was your choice.' I am not moved.

She winces in pain.

'I told you, Waradya. I warned you.'

'I believe my love is stronger than your pain.'

'Who says I'm in pain? I'm enjoying this. Can't you tell?'

She looks up at me in pity. I hate that look.

'If you will not take me with you, then be brave enough to witness what you're pushing me to do!' She says defiantly.

'I don't want to.'

'You must. I won't let you go.'

'You have no control over me!' I bark at her. 'Don't you ever tell me what to do.'

She cries. She runs away. She returns.

She makes love to me.

I fuck her.

Kareem is no longer my friend.

'You have betrayed my trust. You have stolen my daughter's happiness.' He says, despairing. 'What have I ever done but show you kindness?'

'Perhaps I should have let you die in the desert.' I spit back.

'So in exchange for my life you want hers? Is that your bargain?'

'I do not make all the choices, Kareem. She has her choices too.'

'Please leave. You are not welcome in my home anymore.'

I do. I saddle a horse with my possessions. I take provisions. I ride out in the darkest hour before dawn.

I don't say goodbye.

What, you think it's pretty when a soul leaves?

Ha. Think again.

I, Karma, learned how to kill flawlessly and perfectly. Healer turned killer. Bloody hell has no fury like a woman wronged and free to roam and follow the ever burning desire for revenge.

I enjoyed slicing their throats, oh so sweetly and slowly and deeply. I enjoyed how hot, hot blood flowed between my fingers. I enjoyed the screams for mercy and a quick death.

The sound their eyes made when they popped. Like ripe grapes. Pop and juice.

De – light – ful.

Are you sure you want to know about every death? It will make your stomach turn.

Shh, I whispered in their ears, sticking the knife down the windpipe. And then swiftly and with great deliberation, I would make them bleed. And watch them die and give away their soul – eyes glazing over, body slumping, heavy, useless.

The one I burnt alive.

The one that I skinned – he lived to see half of his muscles and two tendons being cut. Screaming music in tones unheard of before. Higher than castrati, fiercer than soldiers in the heat of battle. Pure, sharp, exquisite pitch of pain.

My ribs took time to heal.

My nose - the sharp pain became dull and constant and eventually disappeared.

The swelling eyes and jaw subsided, my face pretty again.

As I learned and fed and studied their scrolls, a plan formed.

How does one go about killing a hundred soldiers?

First of all, I needed to get used to killing fast and quietly. Done.

Second, I was clearly outnumbered and as they had already proven to be better fighters than I – I had to learn their tactics, training and ways. Done.

Third – I had to remain unnoticed for as long as possible. Done.

How does one weasel her way into a company of soldiers? One joins them as a prostitute, of course.

'Death is not the end. The moment you choose destruction, it follows you, like a shadow. And the things you held most precious – love, family, joy – have no more room to grow within.

A life where you cannot love is what hell is all about.'

Letters

Chapter 9 Close

Waradya

I am lying in bed, wrapped in a scarf she used to wear and left behind. I stopped crying at some point. I'm aware of voices outside. I am dying. I am being torn apart with longing. The pain. The pain finds no relief in rocking sobs, or the spiced wine Khtur gives me, or herbs. Khtur gives up. 'Let her be,' I heard her whisper to my father. 'Only time can heal her. Time and our love.'

She's wrong. I know she's wrong. She doesn't understand. No one understands. I will love her forever. There is no end to this. There can't be. I have given her my heart and my soul and now she's carrying it with her. I am not here. I am with her. There is no life, no place in this world for me except by her side.

I don't know how long I was in the tent, or who came to visit me. I remember eyes, concerned eyes. First Amir's, then my father's, then Khtur's. Someone fed me. Someone gave me water to drink. Someone changed my clothes. I did not care. I was not there.

Father wakes me in the middle of the night.

'Wake up, my rose, wake up.' He shakes my shoulders. 'Wake up, my life.'

I focus my eyes on him.

'Come with me.' He says.

I do not understand. Slowly, his words sink in.

'Get up. Get dressed and come with me. I want to show you something.' He orders in that voice of his. That voice I'm used to obeying.

'No. Leave me alone.' I turn away from him.

I hear him crying. He wipes tears from his eyes.

'You are the only thing left to me after your mother. You are the joy of my heart. I can't watch you die. Please, come with me.'

It breaks my heart to hear him cry. I sit up to hug him.

'Don't cry daddy. Please. Not you.'

He presses me close against his body. Sobbing.

'Ya Waradya, apple of my eye. I am afraid for you. I am afraid of what you did and what you have become. All happiness left you.'

He pulls back and holds my face in his hands, looking into my eyes.

'I will not let you die, you hear me? I will not let you give away your life for someone who doesn't want you.'

I weep. He wipes my tears and takes me by the hand.

'Come.'

I follow him. We walk slowly out into the night. Everyone is asleep. Even the crickets are silent.

Outside the village we walk up a dune where the thorn bushes are.

'I met that woman and we spoke of a burning bush.' He begins soberly. 'We spoke of the meaning of our names.'

'Father, what are you talking about?'

'Just listen. You will understand when I finish my story.'

I sit down, looking at the stars. He lowers himself next to me, one arm around me.

'I know you think your life is over. I know you think you are meant to be by her side. But listen to me, my precious daughter. Life is bigger than our thoughts. It is bigger than our feelings. That which moves us all has a plan. And that plan is your happiness.'

'Oh daddy, how can I be happy without her?'

'You loved.' He looks at me smiling.

I blush.

'You loved and love is always a gift.' He pauses. 'But I have good news for you.' He presses my palm into his. 'If you loved once, you can love again.'

I keep silent. Something about his words makes me heavy.

'Wouldn't it be wonderful to love someone who loves you back?' He asks.

'Like you and mother?'

'Like your mother and I, yes, but even better.'

I don't know what to say. When we get back to my tent, I feel very tired. I lay down to sleep. He holds my hand, never leaving my side. The next morning, I eat breakfast.

Regulus

'Onix, please ask Titus to come to my tent and bring his men.'

Onix stands up to his great height and with a sombre nod, leaves.

It doesn't take long for them to arrive.

A map is spread on a makeshift table with the outline of a terrain.

'Come, I want to show you something.' I tell them without looking up.

I point to a location marked by a pebble.

'This is Rome. Where we came from.' I trace a route with my finger winding through the mountains down to the edges of the desert. 'This is the way we came.' I point to another pebble on the map. 'This is our first challenge. A fortified city. Warriors. Their king is already preparing for battle.'

'How far away is it?' Asks Titus.

'Twelve days' journey for the army. Three days for a swift rider.'

'How do you know this?'

'He sent a messenger this morning asking us to either avoid his territory or go back.' I say.

'What did you do with him?'

'I cut off his head.'

This makes Titus laugh.

'Bold move.'

I look at him and his men.

'No matter our differences, we have a task before us. Expand our empire and serve our king.' I say. I look at the aquilifer, the oldest and most experienced soldier in our legion. 'What is your council?'

'We do what we do best,' he says. 'Conquer. No matter the cost.'

Titus interferes.

'Do we know how many men this city has at their disposal?'

I reply. 'I've sent out scouts to find out.'

'Good. We must prepare. I will double the training hours for all soldiers till the scout comes back.'

'Yes. Do.'

'We must start building catapults to launch javelins. And send out a messenger to Rome.'

'I have already given the orders.'

Titus asks, irritated.

'If you've already done everything, why have you called me here?'

I am not impressed with this outburst.

'You are my second in command. We are about to do some serious battle. I am informing you of our strategy in order to win.'

Titus is silent.

Finally, he asks. 'How long till the scout comes back?'

'Three days.'

'Good. We shall re-convene then. Keep me informed.' He says with authority and storms off.

That child.

Chapter 10   Smoke

Karma

Camp lights twinkle in the distance, fires casting shadows on the tents surrounding them. The legion is now within my reach. There they are, the men that destroyed my life.

I breathe in the chill of the autumn night. It's a time of completion – leaves curling up, drying out, falling in their final dance. Everything that buds in spring, drops its fruit in fall.

I feel weary. All the preparation, all the nights setting my intent firm, my purpose unshakable, all the training and the killings and the learning culminates here. On this hill. Regulus. Titus. The Roman soldiers. Men who pillage, rape, and destroy in the name of the empire. That monster they serve with their lives, with their conscience, with their souls. Do they remember killing us, I wonder. Do our screams haunt their dreams? Do they feel remorse? Do they feel?

I take another drag from my pipe, smoke filling my lungs. I exhale slowly, tasting the flavour of the plant between my teeth, on my tongue, through the nostrils. The fire in my belly rages, smoking out and around me. My fury is cold. My will is merciless.

The plant extends its effect through my limbs and muscles, I relax into a smile. All my sisters and my children are dead. I have walked after the men who killed them leaving a trail of dead bodies in my wake. Here I sit, contemplating doing the same thing. Killing. Enjoying it. I will act the same way these men have acted only to me, my actions are justified. I feel good about doing what I'm about to do. I feel they deserve it. I feel I am better than these men. But I'm doing the same thing. Ha.

My head feels light. Thoughts rush through my mind and I see that which is beyond reality.

Feelings are just slight energies on an impassive plain of complete non-judgement that lasts forever. A field where there is no right or wrong – a field where either action or non-action have the same value and the same ultimate result.

Live or die, do or be, say or not, write or not, it does not matter.

Both movement and stillness are essentially the same – completely subjective concepts wholly dependent on the parameters of time and space.

Stillness compared to what? Movement compared to what?

Movement without time makes no sense. There is no movement without time. And if time is really an illusion and the past, present and future all exist at the same time then there is no such thing as movement or stillness.

What a relief!

So from the perspective of no time, Karma and the soldiers are one.

All conversations are taking place at the same time.

All actions and non-actions happen at the same time.

Karma doesn't exist and exists at the same time.

Feel tenderness for life because this consciousness that lives time doesn't often remember eternity.

And sometimes music that plays on these heart-strings of mine reminds me of those moments in time that are only memory.

Music is magic – it is the language of the universe and all that exists.

All that exists and doesn't is tied by time and music.

'In order to cover the whole world in darkness, choose darkness within.

In order to bathe the world in light, choose light within.'

Letters

A freaking bird woke me up with its chirping. I roll over to the other side, burying my head under the mantle, trying to ignore the sound. I can't. It's too damn cheerful.

I sit up rubbing my eyes and yawning. What am I doing today? Right, revenge. Murder. I go to the top of the hill and look down at the camp. They're setting themselves up to move again. I imagine going there, enacting my plan and my whole body sags. This is so not happening today. I really want to go back to sleep. I'm thirsty. I'm hungry. My mind is foggy.

Growling with frustration, I walk back to my campsite. You know what? I'm done with sleeping on the ground and stinking to high heaven. Revenge doesn't have to be so freaking miserable. I said I'm going to enjoy it and I will. Besides, it's really hard to seduce a man when you haven't had a bath in two weeks.

I need a city. I need a guest house. I need a hot meal. I relieve myself in the embers of the fire. Feel better.

Back to the hill. The garrison is moving along the road, sending scouts ahead and messengers to Rome. Their pace is slow. I can outrun them. I can and I will. Till I find a decent town. Rest then revenge. In that order.

Two days later I dismount at the entrance of a cemetery outside a walled city. The tombs are rough stone, engraved with names and epitaphs. The sun's just begun to set to the west, casting a chill over late flowers in bloom. I have my last cold meal of the day at the foot of a beautiful marble relief, depicting a smiling mother surrounded by children. 'Eulalia, mother of a brood of brave soldiers.' The inscription reads. Even carved in stone, she looks slightly worried.

Cross Road Tavern is a place of bountiful provisions and is abuzz.

'Oh mistress, we are in such a fright these days!' The maid servant tells me.

'Atticus, our king, is dead. There's an enemy at the gate. My family is moving away before they attack. I do hope you're not planning to stay for too long.' She keeps fluffing the pillows. 'It is a pity, there's much to see here. The market on Sunday has been planned for weeks and now we can no longer have it. I really wanted to go! My fiancée was going to... '

I interrupt. 'Tell me more about Atticus.'

She pauses to collect her thoughts.

'A more generous king has not been seen for generations. He has done much good, much good for the city.'

'Did he die of old age?'

'Yes mistress.'

'Who is to be crowned next?'

'His son, but he is much too young to bear such burdens. He has his father's generals, of course, but it is not the same. I really don't know what's to become of us. Such dreadful times!'

'Indeed. Have you slaves for sale? And a litter? Where can I buy silks?'

She is surprised at my lack of worry. Replies slowly.

'My cousin is a trader, he can give you silks. He'll be grateful for your patronage. No one buys silks in times of war.'

'And slaves?'

'The slave market is closed. All the able slaves are to fight.'

'I'll pay double.'

She eyes me sharply. 'There are no slaves for sale.'

'I see. I'll be happy to accompany you to your cousin's house as soon as possible.

Have you a litter?'

'Yes, I will arrange it.'

'Thank you.'

When slaves are not for sale, they are there for the taking. Her cousin had four. Her cousin did not live to see the war.

'Water cleanses, water purifies, water is the beginning of life. When the gods and goddesses first saw the Earth, they were happy to find so much water. What a place for life! They said, What a place for creation! They exclaimed to each other. What a wonderful place!'

Letters

Cytheris

Cytheris lays out her pipe and brings out a pouch with dried herbs from a trunk in the corner of her tent. Onix is due to arrive at any minute. She smiles to herself in anticipation. They met when Regulus overtook his company and captured them as slaves; the girls were sent back to Rome as booty to be sold in the slave market, the earnings going to Regulus' family. Onix was tall and strong which is why Regulus must have decided to keep him in service. Perhaps he anticipated some trouble and needed protection. Onix was a strange slave. He did not fight or oppose his capture. Instead, he made himself useful and watched. Jokingly, he said it's like a play that the goddess decided to engage in. I am honoured I can take part.

The tent flap opens and Onix bends on the way in.

'Cytheris, you look lovely. Blessings to you.'

'Blessings to you,' she replies. 'What news do you have? Are we to stay here or prepare for departure?'

Regulus has heard news of a town two days' distance from here that he hopes to conquer. He sent scouts to investigate who the rulers are. He also sent messengers back to Rome asking for reinforcements.

'So we are to prepare for battle.'

'Yes, but not today. Today we can have some fun.'

'Yes.' She points to the pipe and the pouch. 'I am prepared.'

'Not here,' he says. 'There's a spring in the forest to the West from here. Let's go there. Let's bathe and let's enjoy our afternoon off.'

'What about Regulus?'

'He knows I'm with you. I have his permission.'

'How did you manage that?'

'I have my ways,' He says, eyes twinkling.

They head out into the forest. The canopy swallows them, dimming the sounds of the camp, horses whining, soldiers laughing, tools clamping in the construction of a catapult.

'It's so peaceful here,' says Cytheris. 'As if there is no war, no loot, no soldiers.'

'Only men wage war. The goddess is usually at peace.' Replies Onix, pensively. 'This way.'

He leads her deeper into the wilderness, on a winding path that only he seems to see. She picks some berries on the way feeding both. Finally, the sound of the spring edges closer. It runs, murmuring from a hole in the ground into a deep pool of water, continuing out in a thin stream that disappears into the bushes. There is a statue of a goddess by the side, extending her hand in blessing. They both approach and bow in reverence.

'How did you find this?' Asks Cytheris in a whisper.

'It called me.' He replies.

They let their tunics fall to the ground. Look at each other. Smile.

'Ready for a dip?' asks Cytheris, head tilted to the side, teasing.

'After you.' He answers.

She sits on the bank of the pool, dipping her feet in, letting cold water wash away the cares of the days, weeks? How long has it been? She lets the thought go, dissolving in the pleasure of it, the hypnotising sound of water, birds, and leaves conversing. She closes her eyes.

Onyx silently dives in, not wishing to disturb her reverie. He lets the magic of the water take him, too. To another place. The place of freedom that is always within. Here he has no masters and serves no one. Not even the goddess. This is the place where he is who he is, naked and vulnerable. A power awakens within him. Big enough to cause a mountain to explode. He feels into it, body tingling. Takes another dive, approaches Cytheris under water and blows bubbles under her feet. Hears her giggle. Surfaces, wiping the water from his face and extending his arms. She leans in. He picks her and they slowly immerse together. She is too small to reach the bottom with her feet but he isn't. He holds her by her waist, close, wet skin touching.

'Want to dive in?' He asks

'Yes.' She whispers.

'Hold your breath.'

She inhales, puffing up her cheeks. He pulls her with him, down to the bottom, they pause there for a moment, eyes closed, hands exploring each others' bodies. Coming up for air, he kisses her plump, soft lips.

I draw the curtain on this merging of free souls.

Chapter 11 Camp

Auspicious Arrival

'Hey gorgeous! Let papa give you something to suck on.'

'Not sure you'll be impressed with what he has to give you sweetheart. Join us, let's have a laugh.'

'Now boys, don't argue, there's plenty of me to go around.'

'That there is, Cytheris, look at this juicy tit of yours - I could just eat it raw.'

Six men surround her, lust in their eyes.

One of them is playing with a string of pearls.

'Look what I've got from your goddess.' He smirks. 'If you'll be a good girl, it's yours.'

'I'll be a good girl.'

'Hold her steady, boys, I'm going in.'

It lasts a while.

'Whoa, what's the commotion?' The man grunting between Cytheris' legs yells out at the hand that taps him.

'A courtesan is come – she asks to see Regulus and Titus.' Reports a soldier.

'Another one? This is my lucky day! With all the bounty we've collected, I can pay for a high class one.' He says cheerily. 'Cytheris, get out of here, I'll see you later.' He points to another man. 'You, call Regulus! I'll go inform Titus.'

'But.'

'Do it.'

The man rushes off into the main tent to find Regulus and inform him of a strange woman at the gate. She is accompanied by four slaves, carrying her litter. They set it on the ground. Hidden behind thick curtains, he only saw her hand as she passed a letter into the hands of one of the men to be given to the commander. The letter is sealed and the sentinel does not dare open it, it is above his rank.

Everything is confusing these days, the camp in the middle of preparations for battle, the ditch is being reinforced, daily training hours have been increased and the engineers have already finished the latrines and the water supply system. They are no longer on the move. Medics have set a separate tent in preparation for the wounded. Everyone who is on guard duty can see the head of the messenger outside the camp proper, rotting in the sun. It is a constant reminder of their duty to Rome and closeness of death and battle.

The plunging and the pillaging is over. Time for real combat. If they are defeated, there is no going back.

Titus is the first to approach Karma's litter. He bends and opens the curtain. Pauses for a moment and goes in.

Karma

There he is. The sneer on my face turns into a slight smile. The wind blows slightly, making the silk of my tunic leave nothing to the imagination.

'Good day.' He says.

'Good day.' I answer.

I wait for him to speak. He's not in a hurry. His gaze slams into my breasts, nipples painted red. He licks his lips, puffs out his chest, and climbs in, sitting himself next to me.

'A beauty such as this all Rome should worship. What is your name, oh goddess born?'

'Eulalia – you are too kind. I am sure you have among your conquests many women more beautiful than I.'

'That is impossible.' He peers at my face – 'Have we met before?'

'Perhaps.' I say. 'At some feast or other.'

'Hard to believe.' He says. 'I would remember.'

How easy it is to fool men with a bit of powder. My smile stays put. I even giggle.

'So kind of you to pay me such a compliment.' Then in a soft, sweet voice – 'I dare not ask for entry into a caster, I see you are preparing for battle.'

'We are. I am surprised to find you here.' He takes me in, the tunic, the golden bangles, I hear him breathe in my scent, sweat mixed with musk, Bianca used it to drive lovers into a frenzy.

'Oh, I did not mean to cause surprise.' My hand rests on his, I take a deep breath, chest rising. I continue 'My slaves have been running for two days without rest. All the villages on the way to that town have been left empty. I would have kept them running, but I fear they'll die and then I'd have to walk and I so dislike walking.' I say pouting.

He laughs. I giggle, breasts shaking.

At this moment the curtain is pulled back sharply, Titus turns around, quick, coming face to face with Regulus who quickly assesses the situation looking from Titus to me and back to Titus.

I lower my eyelids, placing the hand I had on Titus to my chest, bowing.

'Good day.'

'Good day, my lady, welcome.'

'Regulus.' The look Titus gives him tells me everything I need to know. I watch the two of them battle it out without words. Who gets to go first, I wonder.

Finally, Regulus breaks it off with.

'I read your letter, madam. You may rest and replenish your supplies under our protection.'

'Is this a trading camp?' I ask.

'We are in short supply.' He gives Titus another look. 'I'm afraid our men have not been very kind to the local populace.'

'I am certain we can find whatever she requires among our bounty.' Says Titus.

Regulus changes his tone to an order. 'Please ask Onix to set up a tent next to mine, our guest must surely be tired. And tell him to set a meal.'

Titus climbs out of the litter and walks off clenching his fists.

Regulus watches him depart then turns to face me.

'Forgive my sergeant, he has been in battle too long and forgets his place. I am Regulus, commander to this bunch of savages. May I ask your name?'

'Eulalia.' I say sweetly. 'I greatly appreciate the protection of a centurion led by legendary Regulus.'

'At your service, madam.'

He clears his throat.

'Have we met before?'

'I haven't had the pleasure of your full acquaintance yet.'

The promise in my eyes makes him impatient.

'Please.' I say pointing to the now empty seat next to mine. 'Let us converse while your orders are obeyed.'

'I'm afraid duty takes me elsewhere for now. Will you give me the pleasure of your company after the evening meal?'

'It would be an honour.' I say bowing.

Regulus

He is clean shaven and has recently taken a bath. His hair is still wet. There are oil lamps set on the floor, casting an even glow on his bed, made of bales of straw with linen blankets covering it. The bedroom is separated from the office by a makeshift curtain, raised now. The light in the bedroom is brighter, a stool is set by the bed with wine, cheese, and fruit.

The main room is lit by a lonely lamp set beside a large map on a table.

'Eulalia, welcome.' She is quiet. Only the tingle of her bracelets alerts me to her presence. I turn to face her entrance. She doesn't disappoint.

'Thank you.' She looks around. 'This is quite a spread.'

'I must confess I miss refined company, we've been on the road for too long.'

'And here I was thinking men of war did not know how to treat a woman.' She smiles, approaching the food. 'You have outdone yourself.'

I pour wine into two silver cups. Hand her one. We drink in silence.

'Delicious.' She says. That smile. 'I've been travelling for so long, it seems! Back and forth, town to city. It's exhausting.' She sits on the edge of my bed.

'What brings you so far from home?' I sit right next to her, thighs touching.

'Well all this war and conquest whets the appetite for love.' She says, leaning into me. 'I'm looking for a way to extend the influence of my craft. I left a few girls, just coming of age back in Rome, hoping to find a new house for them in our expanded territory.'

She looks up at me. 'No one is more grateful for female company than men who've seen bloodshed.'

'Yes, war is very good for business.' I'm intrigued. 'Are you originally from Rome?'

'Unfortunately, no.' She replies, face falling. 'The Sabine tribe, conquered by your grandfather, many years ago.'

'Great-grandfather.'

'Yes. Forgive me. I forget my history sometimes.'

'Nothing to forgive.'

I look at her blushing. She seems so vulnerable, so out of place here. It hits me then. What conquered territory?

'Where did you say you are travelling from?' I say as softly as I can.

'Oh, a fortified town, two day's journey from here. They are preparing for war. Every able bodied man in the city is spending money on armour and equipment. No time for elaborate feasts.' She pauses. 'My kind of services require refined tastes. I do not deal with base desires.'

I am torn. I need more information on the town. I also want to know more about her services. Duty comes first.

'Did you happen to notice exactly how many men are buying armour?' I ask.

She looks at me. Smiles.

'You wish to know about your enemy.'

It's not a question.

'I must if we're to win.'

'I did not expect to meet a fellow strategist on my journey.'

'Not many of us walk the earth. The burden of leadership is heavy.'

'I am good at removing burdens.' She says, warmth in her voice.

Who is she?

'You can start by removing my doubt on the number of men on my enemy's side.'

'I would be betraying a long time lover.' She replies and falls silent.

What is she doing here?

'Betrayal is not in your nature?' I ask.

'There are two things of value in this world.' She replies. 'Trust is one of them.'

'What is the other?'

'Love.'

This makes me laugh. Women. So sentimental. She laughs with me.

'Love is but a figment of the imagination. I have not seen love that does not fade with age. The Greek theatres are full of plays of misplaced love. It always ends in tragedy.' I don't know why I feel so strongly about this.

'No matter the ending in the plays or other people's lives. Only true lovers know its worth. No one else can know. It is eternal.'

What is going on?

I clear my throat.

'So you will not tell me of the men because you loved?'

'That love has ended. He is dead. Only trust remains.'

'Loyalty to a dead man? From a courtesan?'

'Loyalty to a memory of what was once whole and holy.'

'You don't know, do you?'

'I know this. Those who decide to win, do.'

I seize her up. Women don't talk like this. What else is she hiding?

'And this dead lover of yours, what was his name?'

'Atticus.'

This startles me. Atticus' messenger serves as food for the buzzers outside camp. This means they are choosing a new leader. This means they will attack later than expected. This means I have more time. I need more information. She is proving difficult. I decide to change tactics.

'You truly do honour to your name, Eulalia. I have not met a more soft spoken woman.'

'One of my many talents.' She smiles, an offering in her eyes.

I decide to take her offer. Lean in for a kiss. She knows how to kiss.

'Chess is a game of kings. The game ends when the king is dead. The piece with the most power is the queen.'

Letters

Karma

He is starving for relief. The burden of warfare is heavy on his lines. Grief darkens his eyes. He doesn't trust me. Yet.

I make myself available, soft and yielding to his every push. Down, down I draw his passion out, slowly. My lips perfumed by wine, he bites into them. My tongue, flavoured by cheese is being sucked of all its nectar.

He moans, remembering what it's like to be nourished.

He pulls himself up, wide eyed, looks into my eyes.

'Who are you?' He whispers in his most sincere voice, underneath the leader's mask.

'Yours.' The sound comes from the base of me, opening.

He sits back on his knees, pushes my thighs out wide and stares, slowly approaching, mesmerised.

I arch my back, my hands find his and let go.

He's good.

I don't show him Karma. Karma is buried under Eulalia – the perfect lover.

I ride him. Straddle his thighs close, pushing him higher, lowering myself slowly.

Squeezing. Every. Step. Of. The. Way.

Yeah.

I'm good.

The point of this is not union. The point of this is information.

My sandals are a work of art. Khtur had them made for me. The left one has an inner pocket for a sheep's intestine, cleaned out, dried in the sun and well oiled. Courtesans don't have babies. The right one has a holder for my dagger, snakes entwined. It rubs against my skin with every move, reminding me why I'm here.

As if I needed a reminder.

He's close. I pull the skin out and dress him up nicely. Smiling all the way.

Time to test his fears, carefully.

I pull back a little, imagine myself somewhere else.

Panic at being abandoned slams into me as he gets up and embraces me close, sucking on my breasts.

I see. Good.

I kiss his brow and hug him back, comforting.

The image of Titus in my thoughts as I look into his eyes.

His thrusts become angry, aggressive, he slams me on the bed, mounting. I push back against him, meeting his anger with mine.

Careful.

I explode. Oops. Did not expect this to feel so good.

He is very pleased. He giggles.

'Oh Regulus, you are amazing.' I croon.

'Ready for more?'

'Oh yes.'

Picture of a soldier wounded in battle.

He softens immediately. Uh oh.

Blushing, he tries to pick himself up. It's not working. He is frustrated. First wave of fear – failure. I see. Good.

I take his hands in mine and kiss them, he is too embarrassed, he's not looking at me. I pull his chin up as I kiss his fingertips one by one, absorbing the fear. Moan.

The discovery lasts all night long.

'Innocence. Return to innocence. Non knowledge. We know not what we are doing. In our darkest hour, we are pure.'

Letters

Ally

I leave the tent at dawn. A whisper. Words uttered by initiates in their first year in training. Ancient words.

'May the goddess be with you.'

'Ever bountiful she is.' I whisper back realising too late that I just gave myself away.

'I knew it! You're a servant of She! What is a servant of She doing posing as a Roman whore?'

'Who are you?'

'My name is Cytheris. '

'Cytheris, how do you know her greeting?'

She falters.

'I was taught. By teachers. You didn't answer my question.'

'I could ask you the same. What is an initiate doing here – I understand your trade is no different than mine.'

She steps back.

'The goddess. Answer my question. What are you doing in Regulus' tent?' She pulls out a blade.

Jealousy. I see. I relax. Come close to her till her blade is right against my skin.

'It seems we're at a crossing of either trust or murder.'

'So it does.'

'You are in love with your patron.'

'You don't know him.'

'Oh yes I do. Better than you.'

'I doubt that. We go back many years. You're just a new plaything.'

'Perhaps.'

We stare at each other in silence.

'I. Please tell me who you are.' She breaks it first.

'A priestess, serving as courtesan, as it pleases the goddess. Who are you?'

'Priestess? Fully initiated?'

'Yes.'

'Which temple?'

'Lilith.'

She shivers.

'The one we passed through?'

'Yes.'

'You survived?'

I spread my arms out in answer.

'Fuck this, I can't do this alone and I'm not about to kill a priestess. I'll trust you.'

'Wise choice. What is 'this'? What are you trying to do?'

'My story is not new. A few of these bastards killed my family, pillaged my home and burned it to the ground. I joined to get revenge. The goddess drives me to spill blood.'

She's lying. Interesting.

'Our purpose is the same, I see. We are allies then?'

'Yes.' She tucks her blade into her belt.

'Then we must speak at length and adjust our plans. How many do you want to kill?'

'There's six of the attackers left. How many do you intend to kill?'

'I want them all.'

'Love is a field. Love begets love. Love is its own reward. The one who loves communes with divinity.

War is a field. War begets torture. War has no rewards. The one who is at war is worthy of compassion.'

Letters

Chapter 12 Love and War

Regulus

'I have received information that Atticus is dead. We are facing a boy king.'

Cato, Titus and several other men are standing around the table looking at the map. More details have been added to the territory surrounding the camp. The forest has been cleared enough to see an enemy approaching from all sides, the wood used to reinforce the camp wall and build catapults.

'And where did that information come from?' Titus asks, smirking.

'A reliable source.' Regulus cuts him off.

'The whore?' Titus and his men laugh.

Regulus is swift. He draws out a wooden shaft and hits Titus with it across the face.

'I have had enough of your mockery. We are at war. I am your commander. You will obey and you will respect my judgement. I will not tolerate disobedience from you or anyone else at this table. Is that clear?' He barks.

Titus steps back, hand on the hilt of his sword.

Regulus stands tall and pronounces slowly. 'Think very well about what you're about to do. I will not hesitate to claim what is mine by right.'

Three of the men move to stand behind him, hands on hilts.

Cato moves to stand behind Titus.

Onix gets up from the ground where he was sitting, sharpening a knife. Step by step he approaches Cato and Titus, unnoticed by either of them. The air is thick with tension.

'I am concerned about where you get your information, commander.' Says Titus finally.

'Sire, our scouts are back.' A sentinel runs inside, oblivious.

No one moves. Without looking at the soldier, Regulus orders.

'Send them in.'

Two more soldiers march in, breathing heavily.

'Report.' Commands Regulus.

'Atticus the king is dead. His son is evacuating all the villages between us and the city. They are preparing for a siege. There is talk among his advisers to move and meet us in the field. The young king refuses.'

'Titus,' asks Regulus. 'How would you proceed?'

Titus does not answer for a long time. He stares at Regulus, hatred in his eyes. Finally, he ventures.

'I would attack the city.'

In a calm tone, Regulus replies. 'Wrong. Due to your training tactics we do not have enough supplies to carry out a long siege. The local populace is not friendly and will not deal with us. Word of your pillaging has reached other villages.' He turns to the scout. 'Are they burning their fields?'

'Yes. Fields, cattle, nothing is left on the path before the city.'

Regulus faces Titus and continues. 'Titus, you may be a descendant of Mars but you have no strategy or experience with battle. That is why I am commanding this legion and not you. Your father has made it very clear in our meeting. He will not be pleased with your doings.'

All colour drains from Titus' face.

He draws out his sword.

Onix grabs him in a hold, putting a knife to his neck.

'That was not a wise move.' He says quietly.

Regulus addresses Cato. 'You now have a choice. Declare loyalty to me or be executed as a traitor.'

Cato drops to his knee, offering his sword. 'I am yours to command.' He says.

Nodding, Regulus instructs him. 'Your first order is to strip Titus of all his armour. He is now a prisoner. You are to guard him with your life.'

'Yes, commander.'

'That is all.'

Titus does not fight as Cato strips him of his sword, knives, and helmet. Onix binds his hands behind his back with rope. They walk out into the main street towards the exit. Soldiers watch, murmuring to each other. Even bound, Titus walks with his head held high. He does not wince as he is tied to the post underneath the messenger's head. He stares straight ahead.

The remaining men confer on further action. Messengers are deployed with letters. After the meeting, Regulus sends out word to all the soldiers in the camp to gather outside. They assemble, standing in ordered files, in eerie silence.

With a decisive step Regulus approaches and positions himself in front of Titus, facing his legion.

'Titus Augustus has disobeyed the chain of command. He has been stripped of his post and duty. He is now our first prisoner of war. For his disobedience, I hereby sentence him to one hundred lashes and three days without food. All of you are charged with the duty to watch. Every man will take turns guarding him. Should he escape, the man on the watch will be sentenced to death.'

With that, Regulus proceeds to whip Titus one hundred times. The sound is sharp in the air, falling on skin, drawing blood. Titus makes no sound.

Karma watches, smiling.

Karma

There's a flurry of activity around Regulus' tent. Messengers coming and going from all directions. A new head stands outside the camp, that of Atticus' heir courtier. A diplomat. The boy sent a diplomat to a Roman camp. What an idiot.

It's good. I have some respite from bedroom antics and time to scheme with Cytheris. We don't even have to be subtle about it. She points out the six men she wants dead, I give her poison. By afternoon they are in the medic's tent. The medics, trained to suture wounds and treat the shits and common cold, don't know what to do with the effects of my kind of medicine.

'Eulalia, the men are suffering too much. What have you given them?' Cytheris asks on one of our walks along the camp perimeter.

'I thought you wanted them to suffer?' I say quietly. No one here speaks our language, but I am extra cautious. Only she can hear me.

'Not like this. You said they'll die soon.'

'They will. But first, they will face the weakness of their body and have some time to ponder their deeds in fever and nightmares.'

She is afraid of me. I try to make amends.

'Cytheris. My loyalty to our pact will remain unchanged. If you so wish, I can give you something to make them go quickly.'

'No, Eulalia. You've done enough.'

'As you wish.' I look at her. 'We both have a lot to lose should either break it. The difference between us, Cytheris, is that you still cling to life and I – I do not.'

'Oh Eulalia, what happened to you that was so bad, you will give your life for it?'

I sense the feeling behind her words. 'Compassion. You have compassion for me.'

'I. You helped me get revenge.' She stops to gather her thoughts. 'I lied to you. Those men did not pillage my home. I'm sorry.'

'I know you lied about that.' I watch her squirm. 'You did not lie about the goddess driving you to spill blood. That was true.' I look at her. 'Cytheris, you are a woman dedicated to the acts of love. Why are you here, in the middle of war?'

'My services. Love. This is where it's most needed.'

'I don't understand.'

She explains. 'When men kill, it takes a toll. They don't see it, not always, but it does. I relieve them of it. I take away some of their darkness so they can go home to their wives and still believe in the goodness of life.'

'Yet here we are, in the middle of planned murder. Those six men. Why are they dying?'

'There is nothing left for me to do for them. They have no more light in them. They will come back to a world of peace filled with lust for murder. They will kill again. For pleasure. I cannot, I will not allow that.'

I decide to tell her the truth too. 'I kill for pleasure.'

She is startled but accepts it quickly. 'You kill for something else. You won't tell me of it. No matter. You wouldn't be able to do it if there was no enjoyment in it.'

'Will you have me killed too, Cytheris?'

She smiles. 'I haven't tried to heal you yet.'

'Oh.' I clear my throat. Cytheris. What a surprise. That smirk, I don't like it.

She touches my arm lightly. 'What do you plan to do next?'

'Titus will be released soon.'

'How do you know?'

'Regulus.'

'He confides in you?'

'Yes.'

'Perhaps you are a better companion for him. He never confided in me.'

'Cytheris.' I say standing still. 'There will come a time where I will need your help. There will come a time where I will need you to do exactly as I say, no questions asked.'

She is silent, waiting for me to continue.

'If I confide in you, will you?'

She doesn't answer. Looks away at the camp and at the men going about their chores, training for battle. Finally, she says. 'I will consult with the goddess. I must.'

'So be it. We will speak again tomorrow.'

Titus

Father has done well. He is threatening to send an army as reinforcements in my support of this expedition against the boy king. The boy king who sends out peacekeepers. What an idiot.

'I see you changed your mind about teaching me a lesson in obedience.' I say to Regulus as he enters my prison.

Regulus does not respond to his tone and states simply. 'Your father promised me men to help fight this war. This has nothing to do with you.'

He issues the order to unbind me.

'Oh well.' I say rubbing my wrists. 'Shall we celebrate our reconciliation? I truly bear you no ill will. That whore must really be something.'

'You will refrain from referring to her as whore in my presence. Her name is Eulalia.'

'Fine, fine. Eulalia then. As you wish. What do you say to a celebration? Between Cytheris and her, I'm sure we can have a mighty feast.'

'No feasts. We must prepare for battle.'

'I thought the boy king refused to come face us? Is he still insisting on a siege?'

'He is.' Regulus nods assent. 'We must do everything possible to draw him out in the open. Sooner rather than later.'

'And how do you plan on doing that?'

'I will use your greatest strength, Titus, your will to butcher.'

A gleam comes into his eyes. He raises an eyebrow. 'Yes.'

'You will infiltrate the city in a week. You and your men. In time to open the gates for your father's army.'

'Good plan.' He replies. 'Then what I have is time on my hands. Interesting. What shall I do to entertain myself?'

'Do not pillage any more villages. We have a shortage of supplies as it is.'

'Regulus, you are a bore.'

Titus, you are a child.

'The men need more training. And so do you. I would suggest you focus your attention on that.' With a final nod, he walks off.

To the whore. Something familiar about her. I need to take a closer look. I watch as Regulus pauses at her tent, changes his mind and goes into the command centre. Too busy for fun. Well, I'm not. She's alone. Why goddess, here I come.

'Eulalia.'

She doesn't look surprised.

'Titus.' She says with a smile. 'Welcome.'

'Regulus speaks highly of your services. I came to see what the fuss is all about.'

'The nature of my services extends far beyond the mere pleasures of the flesh, oh noble Titus.'

I eye her up and down.

'They do? And what else have you got on offer?'

'Fun.' She says putting her finger to her lips, as if it were a secret.

'Fun?'

She smiles. 'War is such a bore. All these men running around, being so serious.

All this talk of honour and duty and strategy. Boring.' The last word, long and teasing.

'I like fun.'

'Do you? I had no idea.' She sits closer. 'What else is to your liking?'

'Pain. Screams. Blood.' I'm curious to see how she reacts.

'I did not expect to meet a fellow thrill seeker on my journey.' She sits up, excited. 'I've an idea. Let's go out and find my slaves and...'

'Madam. Pardon the interruption.' A soldier lifts the flap of the tent. He looks around. 'I did not think you had company.'

'No matter. What is it?'

'Regulus asks for you.'

'Of course.' She turns to Titus. 'Alas. Another time. I must prepare for my patron. Excuse me.'

No, no, no, no, no. Something is not right. She can't just be here on the way to Rome. This, this thrill seeker, as she says.

I have to think about this. She is dangerous. Dangerous whore. What is she doing with Regulus?

Regulus

'When we get to Rome, you must allow me to really throw a feast in your honour.'

'So generous of you! I will be more than happy to attend with all my girls.'

She pours wine for him and her. He is busy admiring her frame. He hands Karma a silver goblet. 'To civilization.' They clink. She takes a sip.

'What news do you have from other fronts of the empire?'

He is surprised.

'A woman interested in war and conquest?'

She laughs.

'It's just me trying to keep your interest. You are, after all, a legendary leader.'

He sits next to her and stares into his silver cup.

'The barbarians are fierce and stronger than we expected. They fight with no regard for their own lives, with a fury that took us by surprise. Rome keeps sending soldiers into battle but it's getting harder to recruit. They raised their pay by extracting more taxes from the citizens. It was not a popular move.'

She nods, all eyes on him. He gets tired of politics.

'Now Eulalia, what arts would you say you excel at? I know that courtesans are always proud of one thing or another.'

'That would be dance.'

'Would you do me the honour of showing me your skill?'

'With pleasure – but I must have music. Do you have a slave that can play?'

'Onix.' He calls out.

'Yes master.'

Please bring your tympanum and play for us.'

Onix enters without meeting our gaze and sits on the floor. She looks at him closely. He keeps his head down. Starts to gently tease the drum. Her body loosens and undulates to the music, the tunic flows with her movement accentuating the curves of her breasts and hips and belly.

Regulus leans towards her – all longing and desire. She cups his chin and kisses his lips. He is so gentle. Skilled.

She yields. Giggles. Stretches. Moans.

Slowly, carefully, he undresses her and lays her on his bed.

His mind is gone – he is focused on penetrating her, leaving her plenty of room to scout out his deepest terrors.

'Ah, yes.'

She slides again.

'Hmm.'

Again.

'Give me more,' she whispers.

Fear of being discovered, fear of death, fear of not being manly enough, fear of his pride being hurt, fear of his wife and her relatives, fear of betrayal, fear, fear, fear. He shows it to her with lightning speed as they push against one another. She absorbs it through her skin, from his eyes and his smell. She rides him harder till he screams out for Apollo, letting her have it all.

'What a blessing from the gods you are, Eulalia.'

'You must have pleased them mightily.'

He spoons against her, inhaling her scent, holding her close.

Onix, still drumming, lifts his gaze and looks into her eyes with awe. He bows his head, promising service. She bows hers in return, acknowledging his seeing.

'In the beginning there was the word, the goddess says. The word made flesh. Am. That word is am. The state of being came before the I. Existence came before separation. And existence was light. Existence was joy. Existence was love. Existence was innocence. Combined to form everything. Containing nothing.'

Letters

Chapter 13 Who do we serve now?

Cytheris

She killed him. If she hasn't already, she will. I know this. I know this like I knew to follow the men on this expedition. I love him. Goddess, I love him. How can you ask me to stand by idly? This is cruel. Too cruel. Goddess, please, do something!

Silence.

No presence.

Is it because I lied about why I was here? Is that why you're punishing me? Oh, please forgive me, I had to.

Cytheris weeps. Deep sobs of remorse and guilt. Turning her head skywards, she pleads.

Goddess, those men I sent her to kill were so cruel when they laid with me. Goddess, they had no reverence for the gift of my body. They did not understand that I took all their pain inside myself. All their grief. All their fear. They did not see that. All they saw is flesh, flesh, flesh. This flesh of mine, theirs to use. They hit me, goddess. They made me lower than dogs. They called me horrible names. They hurt me, goddess.

Silence.

A whisper, heard only by her.

They deserved to die.

She pauses long enough to blow her nose. Doesn't stop the tears, rolling out in a fresh wave of grief and realisation.

Goddess, what did he do to deserve to die?

He did nothing.

I don't understand.

The answer came in images, flashes of statues toppling over, women screaming, men raping. Then.

He did nothing.

Cytheris whispers aloud. 'He did nothing to stop it. He did nothing.'

She gets up and goes over to the bucket of water in the corner of her tent and washes her face. The cool water calms her sore eyes. She goes back to the altar, strewn with flower petals and pretty rocks. Lights incense, letting its sweet smoke spread all around her. She closes her eyes and addresses the deity again.

Goddess, I serve you with my life. I have followed the men as you commanded. I have become a common whore, as you commanded. I have completed my mission here.

Takes a deep breath.

What do you command me to do next?

An image flashes in her mind's eye. Eulalia, kissing Regulus temple, wiping the blood off her blade.

Serve her.

No, that can't be! She's a killer. She has no mercy. How can you ask me this?

More images, Eulalia bathing, Eulalia dancing, Eulalia riding, Eulalia holding a bloody severed head.

Serve her.

'Yes,' Cytheris whispers. 'Yes.'

Onix

Deep raspy voice, my voice, calms the sobbing Cytheris. I hold her in my arms, soothing her with a lullaby my mother used to sing to me when I was little.

She has had a communion with the goddess, she says, and the goddess commanded her to serve Eulalia. Eulalia the priestess. Eulalia the killer.

'Why does it trouble you?' I ask.

'Too many deaths. I am afraid.'

'War will always have the sacrifice of innocent lives.'

'I don't think anyone here is innocent.'

'You are, Cytheris.'

She looks up at me. 'Onix, when I started on this journey, I was. I thought I was serving through my craft. I thought I was helping. But now. Now men are dying and I am involved. Not only that, I am involving myself deeper.'

'How do you think Eulalia got involved?'

'She was a priestess at that temple they looted.'

'She told you this?'

'Yes.'

I sigh.

'I knew that temple. It was famous. The priestesses there did much good.'

She wipes the tears off her face.

'Onix, I think this war goes beyond the players in it.'

'How so?'

'I think the balance of power has shifted. These men here do not see what we see, do not feel the truth underneath words. That is why she will succeed in their destruction. They only accept what is readily visible.'

I look into the distance, letting my eyes relax, my pupils dilate. I want to see. I see the field where the men camp and sit together talking. There are light men and dark men and men who hold both darkness and light within. There are cruel men and kind men. But all the men here are soldiers. All the men here have killed. All the men here are prepared to die in battle. All the men here know they will not return home.

Cytheris shifts and I release my grip on her.

'What do you see Onix?' she asks.

'Men ready to die,' I answer.

'I only want to know how our help and our path is of service here.'

'You mean love?'

'Yes. Love. Compassion. Healing.'

I hold her by the shoulders, and look deeply into her eyes.

'Cytheris, when war and destruction are the order of the day, our service is the only thing standing in the way of complete annihilation. If there is no one holding love, the world will perish in darkness. I cannot allow this. We cannot allow this.'

We sit in silence as she nestles against me. I rock back and forth, going back to the lullaby my mother used to sing to me.

'How can we love more, Onix?' She asks finally.

I smile. 'By reminding those who do good of who they are.'

'She's not doing good.'

'Not yet. That's why we're here. To remind her of who she is.'

'I just hope she's not too far gone into the abyss.'

'I hope so too.'

'There are no winners in war. There are commanders and soldiers. There are interests of the state and interests of individuals. Above all, there is the interest of darkness that divides.'

Letters

Men

'Hey, you.' A soldier booted another sleeping on the ground to wake him up.

'Get the fuck away.' The man said and huddled under his blanket.

He was booted again.

'Get up, it's your turn to stand guard.'

'Says you!' The man lifts his head to argue back louder. 'Get away from me. I serve Regulus, not your filthy man whore Titus. I only obey Regulus commands.'

The boot didn't move. Then disappeared for a few moments followed by a bucket of cold water being spilled on his head.

'Get up,' I say.

'That's it! I'll kill you!'

He gets up, the booted man stands back. Blades out, they start fighting, sparring and defending.

'Ho, wait! What's the commotion? What's the meaning of this?' A fat man comes out of his tent, his voice sharp, used to obeying orders.

They stop and turn towards him, saluting. 'Sergeant!'

'He didn't want to stand guard.'

'He woke me up with a bucket of water on my head.'

'He refused to...'

'Shut up, both of you. You,' the fat man points to the soaked man. 'Go change and stand guard.'

'But.'

'Obey now or you will be hanged.'

'Yes, sir. Yes, Cato.'

'You, he turns to the other one. You will be lashed ten times at dawn for inciting warfare within the camp.'

'But.'

'Obey or you will be hanged.'

'Yes, sir.'

They both salute again and leave in opposing directions.

'What happened?' Another sergeant approaches.

'They are restless. Their loyalty to the unit is wearing thin.' He turns to face the man. 'Unless we find a common enemy to unite them, there will be more and more fights like this.'

'What can we do? Our leader is sick.'

You must speak to Titus. Tell him Regulus is about to have a mutiny on his hands.

'Aye. I think he might like that.'

'I fear he might.'

They stand in silence for a while.

'What do we do?'

'We stand back and watch it play out. There's enough bounty here to take back to Rome and retire rich. I intend to retire rich.'

'What if there is a mutiny?'

'Keep our unit close. Defend against the rest. If you get separated, meet with us at the western edge of the forest. We'll head back to Rome. Tell only our men, no one else. Understood?'

'Yes.'

'Go now.'

The man hurries away, his footsteps echoing in the night. The fat man goes back to his tent.

Another soldier pokes his comrade awake.

'Lucius, get up.'

'What is it?' He answers sleepily.

'Sh, don't talk too loud.'

Lucius, wide awake now, raises himself on one arm.

'What is it, the enemy?'

'No. A traitor.'

'A traitor? Who?'

'Sergeant fat face.'

They are both silent for a moment.

'What should we do?' Asks Lucius.

'We should tell Regulus immediately.'

'Are you sure? Onix isn't letting anyone in. And he's with that courtesan all the time.'

'If we don't, our commander will be betrayed by his most trusted man.'

'How is that any of our business?'

'Don't you have any honour?'

'What honour? They're paying us to be here. If we want to keep the pay, we better stay alive.' Says Lucius.

'But we must tell him. What if it saves his life?'

'Save your own life, you idiot. I'm going back to sleep.'

With that, Lucius turns on the other side and goes back to snoring.

The soldier lies awake for a long time looking at the stars. Should he tell Regulus about what he's heard? What if he's wrong? What if he misheard the information? What if the sergeant is there and denies it? He'll be executed for treason. He sighs deeply.

'None of my business.' He mumbles and goes back to sleep.

Chapter 14 The importance of keeping face

Titus

'Titus, what is ailing you? Have a drink with us!'

'I am worried about our commander. The courtesan has him wrapped around her finger.'

'The bitch must have a pussy filled with honey.'

'You laugh but when was the last time you've seen him in training? We've not moved camp for a week now.'

'It's the sickness, remember? We're stopped till our men recover.'

'When have we ever stopped for anyone? Are you stupid? Don't you see? It's her influence.'

'Oh come on, she's only a whore. Do not imagine her being more than she is.'

'Onix,' I catch him going somewhere. 'Bring me more wine. And tell Cytheris to come to my tent.'

'I think he wants her to wrap him around her finger.' I hear.

Laughter.

'What did you say?'

'Nothing.'

'Come back and repeat it to my face.'

'I didn't say anything, I swear.'

'Come here, I said.'

I reach the soldier in three strides. Put a dagger to his neck.

'Repeat your words.' I hiss.

'I was just saying you want the courtesan to yourself. Anyone can see that.'

'You worthless pig.'

Rage drips blood from the soldier's neck. He falls to the ground, trying to stop the flow.

Eulalia watches.

I catch her gaze.

She smiles at me, nodding a greeting.

Bitch.

'As above, so below. Everything moves in patterns, rhythms spiralling. We are all part of it. Every single nook and cranny of ourselves. Every act, thought, and feeling. Whirling in the dance of life.'

Letters

Cytheris

Cytheris is sitting at her evening meal. The camp is noisy with activity; shouts are heard; the clash of swords, men training for battle. So many people with conflicting purposes, it's hard to stay centred. She connects to her core, the earth and the sun, like she used to when preparing for feasts. Onix steps in.

'Cytheris, Titus calls you to his tent.'

His tone of voice puts her on alert.

'What mood is he in?'

'Suspicious, of Eulalia. His men mock his seeing but he will insist. He asked for wine and you.'

'Damn it, that son of a common whore is cruel when he's in a bad mood. Where is Eulalia?'

'With Regulus.'

'Tell her I need advice.'

'Cytheris. Be safe.' He wishes he could protect her and take her away.

'Onix, as you said, our lives are now entwined. I do not know how or why.' She finishes the last bite of fruit and chews slowly.

He stands, waiting patiently. Finally, she looks up at him and gets up from the pillows on the floor.

'I cannot be afraid now. I know Titus. He wants someone to fear him. His dealings with my boys were not kind. Why is he in a bad mood?'

'His men. They tease him.'

'I see.' I fold my hands, ready to accept whatever comes. 'Onix, if I go, I may not survive our encounter.'

'Is that why you are asking for her help?'

'Yes. She knows how to deal with Titus. I choose to trust her.'

Onix looks away into the distance, pondering.

'I'll keep a close watch if she fails you. I will not allow any harm to come to you.'

'You are risking your life.'

'So are you. How can I tell her without alerting Regulus?'

She smiles. 'Tell her the desert wind is coming.'

'Words. Will she understand?'

'Of course. We talked and made a plan.'

'Stay here. I'll be back.' He turns around. 'A plan. How can I help?'

'Stay close to us. Be there. Do not interfere. We'll ask for help when we need it.'

'That I can do.'

Regulus

I will take my time.

Karma is spread out next to Regulus who is drinking, talking. Relaxed. The duties of the day are done and he can have some time for pleasure.

'Oh where is that Onix? I sent him out for more wine ages ago.' She laments.

Onix enters with a sheepskin. 'Apologies. Master Titus wanted a service.' He says. 'Here is the wine you asked for.'

Karma looks up sharply. Regulus says. 'Thank you, Onix. What service did he want?'

'He asked for Cytheris.'

'Ah Cytheris, good woman.' He turns to Eulalia, 'Have I told you about the hills of Rome? They are beautiful indeed. I used to run around there as a boy, before my father..'

'Regulus, darling, you're getting nostalgic, that means you need more wine.' She interrupts. 'You always tell such good stories. Let me pour some for you.' She takes the wine from Onix and asks 'Onix, Cytheris?'

'The desert wind is coming.'

She doesn't even blink. Gets up saying 'I don't wish to spill it' and goes to the table, where a box of herbs she uses has a small compartment for a powder. She pours Regulus a cupful of wine.

'Here, darling, drink and tell me more.' She says coming back to where Regulus lies, offering the goblet with both hands.

He takes a good gulp.

'Wait, wait. I want some too.' She clinks her cup with hers. 'To Rome.'

'Yes, to Rome.' he replies and takes another sip. 'I grew up there then went to school. My old companions. We ran, with friends, the sun on our back.' His eyes feel heavy. 'We swam..... in ponds.... summer... father...' She catches the goblet before it falls and spills over as he passes out. Checks his breathing. Turns to face Onix.

'Onix. Who do you serve with your life?'

'Cytheris asked for help. I stand by her now.'

She studies him and makes a quick decision.

'Quick, tell me, what's happening.'

'Titus grows suspicious of your influence. He asked for wine and Cytheris. She may not survive the encounter. He is cruel when he's drunk.'

She nods assent.

'His men?'

'Drinking by the fire.'

'Send Cytheris to them. She knows what to do.'

'What about Titus?'

'Will you be by my side when I face him?'

'Do you need me by your side?'

'Yes.'

'What are you doing?'

The air is thick with power. They measure each other.

'I serve Lilith.' She answers the question in his mind.

He nods. 'I serve love.'

'Is there room for us to work together?'

'Yes.'

She stands up, approaches him and puts her hand on his shoulder. 'Then lead me to him.' She says.

Titus

'Eulalia! What a surprise! I ask for Cytheris and get the courtesan herself! This means that I was right. You have a game with Regulus! Tell me, whore, what is its purpose? Don't tell me you want to be his wife – he's married, you know and her family holds him by the balls. No, you're too smart for that. What is it then? Riches? Influence? Do you want an introduction to a senator? I can give you that. My family has connections to the senate.'

He is pacing around his tent, the torrent of words a cloud of wine and confusion. Karma stands still. Her words are slow, measured, and calm.

'Titus. I am here by my own will.' She says.

'Oh really? Regulus not enough for you?' He asks, irritated.

She replies. 'Your desire for me has not gone unnoticed, Titus. It puts you in danger. Regulus is a jealous man.'

'Ha, and concerned little you decided to come to the rescue? I don't buy it. No, no, you must have something else up your sleeve.'

She smiles.

'Titus, we haven't had much chance to talk and get to know each other.'

'Cut the crap, Eulalia.' he spits out. 'I'm no fool. Tell me your game.'

'I have no game.'

He gets angry.

'You stroll into our camp like it's festival season.' He yells, gesticulating wildly. 'We stop advancing. We stop waging war. My men start dying of mysterious illnesses.'

Smile fading, warning in her voice. 'You give me too much credit.'

He turns to face her, approaches. His eyes narrow.

'Something about you is familiar.'

'Titus...' Second warning.

'Just be quiet for a minute.'

She bows on one knee, reaching for her sandal. 'As you wish, master.'

He trembles at the words. Loses control. Pounces on her, ravenous. Bites into her neck, slaps her skin. Hungry, hungry. Doesn't notice the dagger sliding into a corner. Slams himself into her, pounding, aggressive, raw.

'You are mine, whore.'

She closes her eyes, jaw hard against the pain.

Fuck.

No holding back now. All traces of humanity leave her and she growls through her teeth into his ear, legs up, building momentum till they both roll over, her on top.

With an 'I am yours, master.' She bites into his lip, drawing blood, riding.

He slaps her, hard, holding her thighs, ramming himself in, deep. She pushes back, harder. The sounds they make, animal. His darkness meets hers, she absorbs his rage, his desire. She covers him with her hate. It engulfs them both.

They scream with pleasure.

Chapter 15 Seamless execution

Titus

After. It was after all the screaming, when the pounding in their ears subsided to a hum and the sounds of the outside world started coming into their awareness. After their breathing changed from animal to human. After they stared at the tent ceiling pondering what had just happened. After they set their next intent. After the fire in their bodies settled. Only after that they sat up to look at each other.

He spoke first.

'Come with me. We can conquer the world.'

She looks at him. Settles deeper into her purpose. Smile spreading on her face she raises her chin and says

'Yes.'

Onix comes in bending on one knee, covering her dagger, slipping it into the fold of his tunic.

'My deepest apologies. Regulus has woken up and is asking for Eulalia.' He informs them, not looking up.

She doesn't answer. She keeps looking at Titus. Smile never leaves her face. 'Onix, please tell Regulus I will be with him soon.' She says. They both wait for him to leave.

Finally, Titus smiles back. 'We need a plan.'

'Yes. What is your plan?'

'Regulus must die.'

'Are you certain?'

'Will you do it?'

'He trusts me. You're asking for a lot.'

'I'm offering the world.'

She decides to test him. 'Let's start with Rome. A house.'

'I thought you had one.'

She holds his gaze, letting the silence grow.

He agrees. 'Fine. You can have a house.'

'A house in the hills.'

He gets angry. 'I see Regulus has been talking.' Gets up and adjusts himself. 'I offer you the world and you bargain with me.'

'I value your offer.' She answers. 'I agree to it. We have the same desire to rule.' Voice low with satisfaction. 'If I'm to stand by your side through every battle we encounter, we must have a solid base.' She lets him think about it. 'Conquering the world starts with a solid base.' She repeats and lets the words sink in.

He gets inspired with the idea. 'I have a house in the hills. It is yours.' He ponders. 'With the bounty we've collected and my father's army, there's nothing that can stop us.'

'Your father's army?' She is quick. 'How many men are at our disposal?'

'Ten thousand.'

'Impressive.'

'As soon as Regulus is out of the way, we can lay waste to the city. We can build an empire that will last a thousand years.'

She smiles. 'And revenue. A lending house.'

It brings him out of his dream. Irritated, he says. 'You ask too much.'

She doesn't back down. 'If we are to conquer the world, Titus, it will require funding. Men. Equipment. Supplies.'

'But that's my job.'

'Yes, it is. Your job will be to march and rule. Mine to make sure our every need is covered. I do not ask for it out of whim. I only wish to serve you.'

'Fine. You can have the lending house in the east quarter.'

'The poor one? You can do better than that.'

He keeps pacing. Stops suddenly.

'I remember you now.'

'Do you?'

'The temple. You were one of the priestesses.'

Live or die, it does not matter.

'Which temple?' She asks, her tone even.

'The one we conquered. A few months ago. Their little charges came to greet us. They fought. You were there.'

'You conquered a temple?'

'Yes, yes. We did. It was on a hill. It was so rich.'

Unflinching.

'Ah, then; we have enough for our first expedition. You collected a bounty, I assume.'

'Yes, well. Yes. So it's not you?'

She shrugs.

'Oh well. I only caught a glimpse.'

Karma reaches out with a gesture.

'About the lending house.'

'East quarter, Eulalia. You're going to have to make it work.'

'Fine.' She nods. 'Will you draw up the paperwork?'

'What, now?'

Patience.

'I am about to go meet Regulus. I'll have some explaining to do. I must protect you from his wrath.'

'I think it's your neck you need protecting.' He laughs. 'Here. A promissory note granting you ownership of the villa and the lending house in the east quarter.'

He writes, hastily. Signs it. Seals it. Hands it to her.

She stands up, adjusts herself, approaches him and caresses his cheek.

'The world is ours, king Titus.'

He smiles. 'Yes.'

'I'll send word soon.'

'Yes.'

The kiss he gave her had no fear in it. Neither did hers.

Regulus

'Ah, Eulalia, I don't know how to repay you for your care. This illness is no sight for women.'

They had been talking and drinking all night. He finally slept, restless, in a fever. By morning he was throwing up in a bucket. Sweating and shivering.

'I received some training in healing, darling. I plan to make you well. Let me distract you from your suffering, are there any new letters to read?'

'Yes, a messenger arrived this morning. Read it to me.'

'It is from your brother-in-law. The king is dead. It is now imperative that you return without Titus or you will lose everything.'

He ponders the letter for a while.

'Titus' father is sending his army this way. I will lose if I have to fight against them.'

'Armies can be bought.' She states.

'I don't know how I will do that if I am dead.' He heaves up again, falling back on the pillows, weak.

'I can help you.' She says quietly.

'What?'

'I can help you.' She repeats, louder.

'Eulalia, I'm not sure what you're saying.'

'Darling, these are dangerous times for a woman to travel alone. If Titus and his family are as powerful as you imply, then if he ever returns to Rome, it will not be safe for either of us. I do not want to end up a slave. I would rather help you ensure he does not return.'

'Eulalia, this makes no sense. His army is already on the way. As long as Titus lives, they will be our allies. If I have him executed, they will turn against me.'

'I did not say you had to execute him.'

He looks at her, uncomprehending.

'Regulus, you are admired among your men. I see how they look up to you as their leader. They will follow you anywhere. Titus has his own men with him but they are outnumbered, for now. You can give the order to eliminate all his soldiers and claim losses to the boy king.'

'Eulalia, I still need Titus to conquer this city. The boy king is not fighting us. We will be discovered.'

She pauses, gathering her thoughts. 'Regulus, have you considered why Titus' father is sending his army?'

'To expand the empire.'

'And who is now the ruler of this empire?'

'I am.'

'Why does he support you and not his son?'

This gives him pause. 'Please continue.' He asks.

'You are both competing for the throne. Titus will soon have a greater army at his command. If he does your bidding, he will conquer the city. For his father's army.' She goes quiet for a moment. 'After that, what will you be left with, Regulus?'

The silence between them grows. The power in the room moves and shifts. He looks at her with new eyes. 'What do you suggest?'

'Remove Titus before his army gets here. Retreat. Come back with Titus' army as your allies and have a successful siege. I will help you remove him.'

'This is a possibility.'

'Yes. Perhaps I am wrong. I am no war leader. You are.'

She pours some water into the goblet and gives him to drink. Adjusts the cloth on his head.

'These are difficult times for you. I will not trouble you with this any longer. You need rest.'

'Wait. Stay. Please.' He reaches out for her hand.

'I sometimes forget how little I know you, my love. You always surprise me. When we're in Rome, I'll shower you with gifts and introduce you to everyone. Your beauty and wit will make me the envy of the capital.'

She sits on the edge of his bed, smiling at the dream.

'Oh yes, I'd like that. And where will we live?'

'You'll have a house that I will visit every day.'

'In the hills? You spoke so much about them.'

'Yes, if you so wish.'

'Oh darling, you are so generous! Thank you. How can I make you more comfortable? What will ease your suffering? Shall I play some music?'

'No, you gave me a lot to think about. Can you come back later?'

'Of course, my love.' She stands up to go. 'Before I go, may I offer one last suggestion?'

He nods.

'Regulus, my love. You are in no condition to do battle. Removing Titus and his men will grant you more time. Time to recover. Time to regroup your men and ensure absolute loyalty.'

'Go on.'

'Set the order to your sergeant. To ensure secrecy, let no one come to your tent that night. I'll arrange for a fire to be started at the end of the camp – that will be the signal for your men to move into action. You won't be involved. It will look like the boy king's sudden attack.'

'This has not just occurred to you. This looks like a strategy you've been pondering for some time.'

She lowers her eyes.

'Our talks on war and politics bore fruit.'

'Eulalia?'

'Yes.'

'What have I done to deserve you?'

'The gods smile on the bold.'

'Eulalia?'

'Yes.'

'Prepare to leave the camp at a moment's notice and return after three days.'

'My love!' She exclaims. 'You have decided then?'

'Yes.'

'When?'

'Dawn. Kiss me.'

He fears failure and death. He fears she will not think him brave or good enough for her. He fears he will never see her again.

Onix

She is lying on her narrow bed of straw, arms out, eyes closed, resting. I clear my throat as I step in.

She opens her eyes.

'Onix.' No more strength in her left. I approach her bed and pour her some water as she sits up.

'Drink.'

After what seems like a long time, she takes the cup and drinks.

'I brought you something you have lost.' I hand her the dagger, snakes entwined.

'Thank you.' She slips it into her sandal. Looks up, expectant.

'We have not had any time to speak at length.' I sit on the floor, legs crossed.

'Now is a good time to speak.' She says.

'I have a skill.' I say. 'My mother taught me how to loosen the limbs and restore vitality to a body. If you will allow me, I will happily offer it to you.'

'You offer me your skill? Why?'

I tell the truth. I know only the truth will do.

'Cytheris is a friend. You prevented her death. You took on Titus for her. This is my way of saying thank you.'

Her gaze, measuring, probing. Finally she states.

'You have seen me with Regulus.'

'You are destroying him.'

'You have heard me with Titus.'

'You are like him.'

I will not be cowed back by her denial. I am here to speak what is. She must see that.

'You have heard about me from Cytheris.'

'I have heard about what you are long before Cytheris. In whispers. Over fires under the full moon. The dark goddess.'

'I am no goddess.'

'That which moves you. That which feeds you. The power of Lilith. I see her in you.'

She drinks more water.

'You know of Lilith?'

'I know of Lilith. I do not serve her, but I know of her.'

'What does love have to do with Lilith? Why has your service brought you to me?'

'That I do not know. Perhaps Lilith deserves to be loved.'

'In all her horror?'

'In all her splendour. In her full power. She who did not submit. She who was cast out into the underground. She whose children are killed. The fear she raises is the fear of chaos. No control. She who has no mate.' He lets the words die down. 'Yes, I heard about Lilith. From my mother, on dark moon nights, talking of dreams and shadows. From my father, telling me to try and find one who embodies her.'

'Your father?'

'He said men only imagine they are powerful. Until they catch a glimpse of Lilith in form. Then that illusion falls away.'

'Your father is a wise man.'

'Was. His name was Daniel.'

She closes her eyes against the memory. Drinks more water.

'Your offering is kind. I thank you. Perhaps another time.'

'Is there anything else I can do for you?'

'Yes. Tell Cytheris to leave the camp, an hour after midnight and walk west. Tell her to set fire to her tent before she leaves. Tell her not to return for three days.'

'Will you need me after?'

'Yes. Follow me to Titus' tent. As soon as you hear moans, enter. I want him unconscious.' She lays the cup of water on the table, puts the dagger back into her sandal and gets up.

'Consider it done.'

Regulus

The light of the candles cast shadows on Regulus' eyes. Dark circles and fine lines frame his face. The gaze he directs at her lights up with love as she enters the room.

'Eulalia,' he says, straightening up on the pillows, smoothing his blanket.

'Yes, my love.'

She approaches his bed and sits at his side, tucking in her ankles.

'Have you sent the orders?'

'Yes.' He closes his eyes for a moment. 'I have made my move.'

He opens them and sits up; takes both her hands into his and squeezes them, urgently.

'I fear I will not live through this night,' he begins. 'I have made peace with the gods.'

'Don't talk like that. You are a king now.'

'No, I fear it's my time.' He pats her hands. 'I want to thank you for making these last days so beautiful, Eulalia. If I live, we will... that will be another world. If I die, I die in peace knowing that even when I'm gone, you will be taken care of. Aside from the house, I have decided to give you all the slaves that we captured during this expedition, including Onix. No please, don't interrupt, I have made my decision and signed the papers. Onix will serve you well. Take my share of the bounty too. As you say, it's a dangerous world for a woman alone. Money will make it easier on you.'

'Regulus, I have no words.'

'Listen to me. My wife hates me. My children despise me. They think I am weak and my notions of honour silly. Then you appear and you see my honour, and you understand me and you hold me close. You are by my side when I'm sick. You comfort me with words and your gifts. Eulalia, you are a blessing from the gods to me. I know this. I don't know why fortune has smiled upon me this way, but I'm so happy it did.'

'Regulus?'

'Yes.'

'I forgive you.'

The blade, thin and precise, fit snugly in its leather sheath against her shin. It is long enough to pierce his heart.

'Shush. It's fine,' she says. 'It will be over soon.'

'Shush.' She whispers, again. Watching his surprise and the look of betrayal in his eyes. 'That's right, don't fight it.'

He struggles, but is too weak against her fist, squeezing the handle. His heart beats its last against cold steel and stops. His eyes glaze over and she watches his final breath go up.

She pulls the knife out, swift and firm, wipes the blood off with the sheets, never taking her eyes off of him. He looks peaceful. She turns him over on the side and covers him with his blanket. Kisses his temple.

'We are done. No more debt between us.'

I will enjoy every kill.

Titus

Titus is drinking red wine from a golden cup decorated with rubies. His eyes sparkle with the delight of a hunter faced with a tiger when he sees her.

'Eulalia,' he places the wine goblet on the table and stands to face her.

'King Titus.' She approaches and gives him a kiss.

'You look pleased with yourself.' He says.

'I fulfilled my part of our deal. Regulus is dead.'

His eyes widen at the news. Gleam with victory – so close. She quickens her breath, making him think of eros and bloodlust.

'Good.' He says, raising his goblet. 'To victory!'

'Yes,' her voice, a whisper, tinged with invitation. Sips at the wine. He puts his goblet on the table, grabs her hair with both arms, pulls her head back, exposing her neck. She breathes faster.

'King.' She whispers.

He licks her neck, gently, shoves his arm between her thighs roughly and buries two fingers inside her. She places a leg on a stool, opening, he buries his fingers deeper. She moans, closing her eyes, letting herself be vulnerable. Her hands on his ears, caressing; her breath, hot against his neck. His fingers move faster; she moans louder to cover Onix's entrance.

Onix is swift. He grabs the golden goblet and hits Titus on the head with it, knocking him out. They bind his arms and legs and gag him.

'Fire!' A soldier screams. Cytheris did her part to perfection – the signal to attack.

Horses whining, swords clashing, men dying. Fear and panic spreads like incense burning.

'Let's move – to the forest.' She says. They head east.

Onix places Titus on his shoulder. She sets fire to the bales of straw that were his bed. In the commotion no one notices them.

'This way.' Karma walks ahead of Onix, swiftly.

They move from tent to tent along the perimeter, the madness of battle all around them. They run past the soldiers, past the fires now everywhere, past the gates, quickly, quickly into the safety of the forest. Deeper, quicker, moving between the trees until the sounds of battle die out and only the owls are heard hunting. They find a clearing with an oak tree and suspend Titus upside down on a branch. He starts to move, moaning.

She looks at Onix. He stands, expecting to witness a quick death.

'Onix, I thank you for your service. Take this.' She hands him the goblet. 'It will be enough for you to travel home as a free man. If you return to camp tomorrow, I'm sure there will be more loot for you to take with you.'

'Eulalia, why? Have I not served you well?'

'Your service has been invaluable. Worthy of a reward from the gods. If this is not enough, tell me what I can give you and I'll do my best to match your request.'

'Eulalia, we spoke but not enough. I know you. My mother was a healer in our tribe in communion with the goddess. Your power reminds me of hers.'

'I do not heal, Onix.'

'You used to.' He pauses. 'Rania.'

She is silent. He can sense the menace in her stance and breathing. Her eyes look into his.

'I do not know that name.' Steely warning in her voice.

He explains. 'My mother had an apprentice. The girl was strong and gifted. Good enough to be chosen by your sisterhood as a novice. I was taking her to the temple when the Romans overtook our party. We were made slaves. I was with them when they destroyed it. I was with them when they defiled you. I do not know how you survived.'

He pauses for breath then continues.

'Rania, my father was there. He trusted your healing. Your gifts were known far and wide. I cannot. I will not leave your side.'

She accepts it. 'So be it.' She nods in Titus' direction. 'I want to be alone for this.'

He starts to walk off. She calls after him. 'An hour's distance should be sufficient, Onix. Come back in the evening. And Onix?'

'Yes?'

'My name is Karma now.'

He nods and disappears into the shadows.

Titus had been listening, carefully. He was watching, alert. For the first time, there's fear in him.

Chapter 16 Dawn

Karma

I hated Titus with a hate that came from the hole that was left by my soul leaving.

I hated Titus with the hate of the agony of a thousand days without my sisters.

The pain that intensified with each day and pushed me forward with the madness of murder and bloodlust.

I hated Titus for everything he represented – the new way, the way of power over others.

Power over others that takes no account of the common good, of what is better for the whole - greedy, dark, fear-based, and egomaniac.

Power over others that feeds on fear.

Power over others that uses sex as a tool of enslavement that binds you. Opens up greed, lust, possessiveness, cruelty, murder, death, separation.

Power over others that brought hell to earth.

Power over others that I entered into because it was the only way to get my revenge.

Power over others that I chose.

Gladly.

Subtle ties bound Titus and I -

I hated him,

I wanted him.

He took everything from me -

He gave me hell to explore.

What a gift!

Titus was hanging from a tree.

He was a bit afraid of me.

Karma, Karma.

Who are you?

Karma, Karma

Whatcha gonna do?

Can you hear my tinkling laughter? This is going to be so good.

Revenge

And I will have no mercy.

Fear. He smelled of fear. Sweet, delicious fear. I bring my face closer to him and inhale deeply.

'Let's talk about this.' He says. 'I can give you money, riches. I can make you the richest woman in Rome! I am king now.' He struggles to escape.

I am not in a hurry. 'You were not very generous when you thought of me as an ally. Why would that change now?' I ask calmly.

He is still blind to who I am. I bring my eyes closer to his. 'Don't you see, Titus? Are you blind? I want nothing but this. You. Screaming. In pain. This is what I want. I thought you'd understand. You like screams and pain.'

It doesn't matter what he says. I take out my blade and cut off a piece of his cheek. He lets out a scream. 'This is what I'm here for.' I repeat.

'You cunt! Let me go. I will set the empire on you. I will kill you. I will destroy you.' He tries to untangle the rope. We bound him well. Knots that we studied at length in our library. Knots that seem easy yet tighten with every move. Tighter; closer; inevitable.

'You already did.' I say. 'My turn.'

The next piece of skin to come off is from his thigh. A long strip, from knee to groin. He screams, spit flying everywhere. Sweat forming droplets on his forehead, dripping onto the ground.

'I trained for years to heal.' I continue. 'I spent days pouring over old parchments on the ways of the body. I made the blind see and the weak walk again. I delivered hundreds of children. I bore five of my own. You cut off my daughter's arm. She died. I couldn't heal her because I was busy fighting your men.'

I cut into the flesh of his forearm, deep, to the bone. I push and pull at the knife, peeling layer after layer of skin and meat and sinew.

'Your men raped us. They defiled our temple and our goddess. They robbed our coffers on your orders.'

With that, I cut into the tendon on his left foot, swift. He jerks, his whole body shaking and shuddering at the pain. The branch holds his weight. Good branch.

When he subsides, blubbering, crying. 'Please, stop. Please. Stop.' I smile.

With a moan he liked to hear so well, I cut his right tendon. His screams reach a fever pitch and he loses consciousness.

I am not done yet. I keep going. I gather some herbs that maintain life from around, kindling for the fire and water from the stream. Onix had not taken the goblet. I use it to brew a strengthening tonic. I need him alive for more.

After I finish preparing the tonic, I slap his cheek, where I'd taken the flesh off. The pain wakes him up.

'Drink this.' I force his mouth open, those points in his cheeks – I used to press them when unruly children did not want to take their medicine. I am not as gentle now. He drinks the warm liquid.

'You see, Titus, I was already rich before you came into my life. You took everything from me. You cannot destroy me because I have nothing left to destroy, Titus. I am already dead.'

I peel off more skin. This time from his chest. One strip. Shudders, pain, exquisite pitch of a scream. Another strip, from his lower belly. Higher than castrati, he screams as my knife cuts into the flesh of his pubis. I can't get enough of his screams. One after another, I peel, revealing muscle. It is deep inside me, pure, lush - his pain. His fear, feeding, feeding my power.

By the time I am done with him, there is nothing left of proud Titus. I cut off his testicles at the very end and throw them into the bush.

His screams finally die and the branch that held him cracks under his weight. He drops to the ground. I sit, watching him. I feel something, something I haven't felt for a long time – I feel complete. I feel a weight lifting off my shoulders.

I lie next to him, watching his blood seep into the grass.

I fall asleep.

I do not dream.

Orders

Onix wakes her up, scared from the blood on her. She sits up and gets to work immediately, cutting off Titus' head. It takes a while, the windpipe and the vertebrae do not give in easily. She twists and turns and cracks the bone and has to cut the marrow. She wraps it in cloth from his tunic.

'Onix, I have a mission for you, if you still wish to serve me.' She looks at him.

'I do.'

'Take this and go to Rome, deliver it to Titus' father. Tell him, Karma is at his service.' She hands him the head. 'Tell him this is a gift. That others can be bought. Do you understand?'

'No. Titus' father? He will have me killed.' He replies.

'Send an orphan as messenger. A street urchin, I believe they're called.'

'I don't understand. Why would he cooperate with you after you have taken his son's life?' He asks.

'He is at war. He will be king. He will get over his grief. Once he does, he will see the value of my service.'

'As you wish.'

'Say it back to me, please.'

'I am to take this to Titus' father. Tell him it's from Karma. Tell him it's a gift and that others can be bought.'

'Good.'

'Will you be living as Karma in Rome?'

'No. If anyone in authority asks you who you are on the way, tell him you serve Eulalia, the courtesan, who will be holding a feast at her residence in Rome three months from now.'

Tell them that everyone is invited, from lieutenant to general to senator. Tell them official invitations will follow shortly. Tell them they are welcome and that I look forward to meeting them all soon.'

Onix is about to leave when she remembers.

'Where's Cytheris?'

'I'm here.' Cytheris comes out from behind a tree.

'It's not true that once you choose a path, you have to follow it till the end.
Choices are made every step of the way.'

Letters

Chapter 17 Best served cold and thorough

Cytheris

There she is, slick with blood, still wet in some places, forming brown flecks in others. She smiles as she sees me and the horror mask on her face cracks. It's terrifying.

'Cytheris. So you're here to continue our pact.'

'I serve the goddess, Eulalia.' I reply.

'I see.' One corner of her mouth lifts in a grotesque smile, the other doesn't. 'And what does the goddess ask of you now?'

'She asks me to be by your side.'

'So be it.' She says. 'The battle will have played out by now. There will be remains on both sides. They will go back to the main army approaching this way. We must catch them before they do. I am not done with my revenge.'

'Is this your way of asking for more help?'

This makes her smile.

'I forget my manners. It's this blood.' She explains, extending her arms out, looking down at her stained body.

'I might know a place for you to wash it off.'

Her eyebrows shoot up in surprise.

'Do you?'

I take her to the spring where Onix and I bathed a few weeks earlier. She nods to the goddess statue by the side and dives deep, washing herself of all traces of blood. Emerges, beautiful, standing naked with her face to the sun, drying off. Her voice is milder this time as she addresses me.

'Cytheris, I know what it takes to serve the goddess.' She begins. 'I know it's not always easy.' Then, after a pause, she looks at me, human again. 'Thank you for being by my side.'

'You're welcome.' I say.

'Onix will set up a house in Rome for me. For us, if you wish to join.'

I let the silence grow.

'There will be a feast.' She continues. 'I want to meet the rest of the players in this war.'

'Why Titus?'

She looks away, not answering.

'Karma, if you want me to help you, you need to trust me.'

'Help me do what?' She is quick.

'Heal. Karma, I begin gently. I heard his screams. I saw you covered in his blood. I saw what you did to his body. I know they destroyed the temple. But this?'

She is silent for a long time. I am patient. I am used to people coming to me in pain. Finally, she takes a chance.

'Cytheris.' She says sitting down, pulling me with her. Continues in a flat voice, with no emotion. 'There were thirteen of us at the temple. Six charges in our care. She names each of the priestesses. 'Mina, Diana, Bianca, Marwa, Berenib, Nimra, Saadia, Aat, Dedeyet, Arina, Livia, Shamal.' She breathes in, fighting back the ball of pain. 'My sisters. Holding the balance.' She trails off.

I let her be. She continues.

'The girls. Leena, Aanaka, Sai, Deena, Sonia, and baby Ruth. They destroyed them. All of us.'

She falls silent again. 'Every cut on Titus' body, every strip of flesh, every scream of his is nothing compared to the agony I felt when he set his garrison upon us. Compared to what it felt to watch them defiled. Compared to what it felt like to watch them burn on the pyre. Everything that I've done to him brought me closer to peace.' She finishes firmly.

'Peace?' I say, surprised.

'Yes. Peace.'

'I understand.' I say softly. 'I will help you.'

One arm

We have been following the soldier's tracks for a week. They were messy and loud, unafraid. It was easy.

'What's our strategy?' Asks Cytheris.

'Well, they know us, don't they?' Karma returns the question.

'Indeed they do, some better than others.' She giggles. 'Divide and conquer?'

'Yes.'

'But how?'

Karma smirks. 'They see us as courtesans, there to serve them. We will serve them.'

'Are you willing to lay with soldiers?'

'If being touched by them can be avoided, I'd rather not be touched. So we're going to appeal to their sense of honour. We're going to appear helpless and needy.'

'Karma, the men in command might have a sense of honour, but these ones will want to get laid. I thought you were beginning to understand.'

'You think?'

'I know.'

'You misunderstand the nature of our service. We'll use poison.' She replies to the question in my eyes. 'We'll cook for them. A stew. Where's the rabbit that you caught this morning?'

I raise it up for her to see.

'We will stick to our story of needing an escort to Rome. We will cook a stew in gratitude.'

'And when they ask for the gratitude of our bodies?'

'We play coy. Shy. Tender and weak.' She muses. 'Until they eat.'

Cytheris asks. 'Have you got enough poison?'

Karma points to her pouch.

'I have enough poison for the whole of Rome.'

'All right then, I'm ready.'

The soldiers were just setting camp for the night. Some building the fire, some letting their sacks fall to the ground, exhausted. One of them saw the women appear and stood up, eyeing them closely.

'Well, well, well, what have we got here? Cytheris! And Eulalia!'

'Oh Cato!' Cytheris rushes into his arms and hugs him. 'I am so glad we found you! We were lost, you see, and tried to find our way back but the forest is so dark and frightening!'

Cato puffs out his chest. Cytheris continues.

'We were getting quite desperate, afraid to be overtaken by wandering bandits or worse!' She screws up her face tearing up. 'Our possessions were left at the camp and we had to hunt like savages! My dresses! My things! Everything was burned! Horrible! Just horrible.' She sobs in earnest.

'Well, well, don't cry now, Cytheris. Calm down.' He doesn't know what to do with tears. 'You're here now. It's safe. We will escort you back to safety, don't you worry your pretty head about a thing.' He pats her on the shoulders, lust in his eyes.

Karma interferes, approaching Cytheris.

'Oh thank you, noble Cato.' She shows him the rabbit. 'Please, allow us to repay your kind service by cooking up a stew from this rabbit. It is the least we can do to show our gratitude.'

'Oh, there are many things that occur to me that you can do.' A soldier pipes up, jeering.

'Shut up.' Cato cuts him off. 'Don't you see they have had enough trouble?'

He looks at both of them.

'There will be plenty of time for that later, eh?' He winks at Cytheris.

Cytheris sniffles and says meekly.

'Oh Cato, we will cook you the best meal you've ever had, won't we Eulalia?'

'Oh yes!' Replies Eulalia enthusiastically. 'You've never tasted a stew such as this!'

'Brr. It's gotten cold all of a sudden.' Says one of the soldiers. 'Men, let's get that fire started, let these ladies do the cooking for us.'

Soon enough the fire was crackling merrily and men were drinking wine in anticipation of a hot meal. The smell of cooked rabbit, wild garlic and herbs disguised the scent of poison. It spread around, making mouths water. No one was looking at their hands, chopping, throwing herbs into the pot. No one noticed the vial, emptied into the boiling liquid. One of the soldiers approached Cytheris from behind, grinding his hips against hers.

'Oh Cytheris, I love how you stir that pot.' He joked to the roaring laughter of the others.

'Hold your horses, my dear. I'm not finished yet.' She laughs teasingly.

'Oh but when you are, I want to go first.'

Cato looks at Eulalia.

'That's all right, soldier. I've got bigger fish to fry.'

'Aye, much bigger fish you're roasting tonight, captain. A fish that bedded the future king himself!'

Eulalia smiles that half smile of hers and approaches Cato. Places her hand on his broad shoulder, gently. In a lowered voice, filled with promise, whispers in his ear.

'Oh Cato.' She says. 'You better eat up and gather your strength. I have big plans for you.' She lets her arm fall to his crotch. 'And I see you have big plans for me. Good.'

Cato clears his throat, embarrassed.

'This is no common whore, eh captain? This is a once in a lifetime chance, you lucky bastard. The gods smile upon you tonight.'

'Yes, yes.' Replies Cato. He is not used to being so desired.

Cytheris raises herself up from the pot clapping her hands.

A feast worthy of the great soldiers of Rome is ready!' She declares.

Men gather in a file with their wooden cups, filled to the brim with the steaming broth. They eat in silence, mumbling in appreciation. After they are done, Karma takes Cato by the hand and leads him into the forest.

'Wait, where are you going? Can't we watch?' His comrades tease.

'No!' Cato shouts out, fiercely.

She leads him deep into the forest, not looking back at him, her face fixed in a frozen smile.

He pulls at her arm.

'We've gone far enough, I think.' Garlic on his breath, he approaches to kiss her.

She grabs him by the testicles and pulls sharply. He doubles over. Her blade slams into his neck, cutting off the sound. She kicks him with her leg. He falls to the ground. She slits his throat and goes back to the fire, slowing down her approach, watching the men rolling on the ground in pain.

'You poisoned us!' One of them says, mouth foaming.

Cytheris pushes a soldier off of her. His body is jerking in agony. The women stand with their backs to the fire watching them die one by one.

'We are going to kill the next ones in their sleep.' Declares Karma. I have no patience for this.

'Agreed.' Replies Cytheris.

The other arm

They spot the traces of the camp, fresh, a day away, they determine.

'Careful now. We must not be seen.'

They make quick work of it. The soldier standing guard is killed first. He does not hear or see them until it's too late. Their knives are sharp, their hands quick. Two soldiers are killed without sound. The other two make enough noise to wake up the last one.

He sits up. Pulls out his short sword. Guided by instinct, he attacks Karma first. She moves to avoid his blade but it slits her forearm. Blood drips on the ground. Emboldened by her wound he attacks again.

'This is not how I die.' She says.

'Yes, it is.' He lunges, aiming for her belly.

She steps towards him, close enough to plunge her blade into his neck.

'No. You die.'

The soldier falls to the ground, grasping at the gushing wound.

After he falls silent, Cythers asks. 'Should we bury them?'

'No. Let the animals have a feast.'

Karma surveys the scene with the dead bodies; the last remnants of the centurion that destroyed her life.

'Now what?' Asks Cytheris.

'To Rome.' She says.

'Now the game has changed. In the gathering of beings we have decided to get our power back. Each one plays their part to perfection. Every step of the way.'

Letters

END OF BOOK ONE

Acknowledgements

I want to thank my people for supporting the creation of this book. Sergio Montoro and the team at Habber Tec; Raul Bartolome Ruiz - for seeing my gift and encouraging my every step, Leticia Blanco for giving me pointers, Dejana Williams (may you rest in peace) - for refusing to take my doubts seriously; Sarah Angelidis - for bringing the spark of joy and laughter. Julie Masters, Lori Thomas, Ana Otolara - for your unwavering support and devotion. My landlady and fellow writer, Lijia Zhang - for being so impressed and showing me what a writer's life can be like.

To my gentle readers. May this book bring you joy, blessings, and peace. Thank you.

Printed and bound by CPI Group (UK) Ltd, Croydon, CR0 4YY

22/07/2024

01020179-0001